MICHAEL RAFFANTI
71 SONIA ST.

The Happy Hollisters at Pony Hill Farm

BY JERRY WEST

Illustrated by Helen S. Hamilton

GARDEN CITY, N. Y.

Garden City Books

Contents

CHAPTER 1

THE HAUNTED HOUSE

"No MORE TEACHERS, no more books," Ricky said cheerfully. "Please pass the strawberries, Holly."

"Here you are," the six-year-old pigtailed girl answered, handing a bowl of big berries across the breakfast table to her red-haired brother. "But I'm sorry school is over."

As seven-year-old Ricky spooned several berries onto his cereal, he remarked, "I like school, too, but just think of all the time we'll have for adventures this summer!"

"And mysteries, too," his older sister, Pam, added. The golden-haired girl was ten and very smart at detective work.

"Speaking of mysteries," their father spoke up, "how would you all like to go to the auction sale at old Mr. Stone's farmhouse?"

"The haunted house?" exclaimed Pete. He was twelve and had blue eyes and a crew cut.

"That's what they call it," Mr. Hollister replied with a grin.

Mrs. Hollister smiled at this. She was a slender woman with a pretty face and blue eyes. "No matter what the children call it, Pete, the house isn't really haunted. No house is."

"Maybe the barn is, then," chirped up little Sue, the four-year-old and youngest of the five Hollister children.

"Not even the barn," Mrs. Hollister declared as she leaned over to dab her napkin at a drop of milk clinging to Sue's dimpled chin.

"What is the mystery, Dad?" Pete asked.

Their tall, athletic father replied, "It's said that something of great value is hidden among the old relics at the farmhouse. What it is, nobody seems to know, and old Mr. Stone who lived there didn't tell the secret before he died last month."

"Maybe his relatives know it," Pam said.

"His only near relative is an orphaned grandson," Mr. Hollister explained, "and no one around here seems to know where he is."

"Let's go out to the farm and solve the mystery!" Ricky said excitedly.

"Right now!" Sue added. "We haven't had a 'venture since the Merry-Go-Round Mystery." She referred to a riddle the children had cleared up a month before at their school fair.

"Not today," Mr. Hollister said with a chuckle. "The auction starts tomorrow morning at ten. By the way, today's newspaper will print a list of all the things to be sold."

Mr. Hollister rose from the table, kissed his wife and daughters good-by, clapped the boys on the

6

back, and left for *The Trading Post*. This was a store he owned in the center of Shoreham, where they lived. It was a combination hardware, sports, and toy store. The children loved the place and often helped out there.

For part of the morning they played with their collie dog, Zip. Then they had a game of leapfrog on the lawn of their spacious, rambling home, located on the shore of Pine Lake. But after Sue took a header over Ricky's back, the game ended.

All the children eagerly waited for the afternoon newspaper, the *Eagle*, to be delivered to their front porch. They wanted to read about the auction.

"Here it comes!" Pam cried and hurried to get the paper from the delivery boy.

Her brothers and sisters crowded around as she looked for the auction ad.

"I see it!" she exclaimed.

Under the heading AUCTION SALE SATURDAY AT STONE FARM, Pam pointed to a long list of articles to be sold. It was printed in small type. The articles included farm machinery, pots, pans, chairs, tables, a clock, butter churn, copper kettle, dinner bell, and many other odd furnishings. Finally Ricky's eyes lighted on something of special interest.

"Look!" he said. "A large rocking horse!"

"A rocking horse for you?" Pam asked, giggling.

Ricky shook his head, then whispered into his sister's ear so Sue could not hear, "Maybe we can get it for Sue."

"Maybe we can buy the rocking horse for Sue."

By this time the little girl was tired of looking at the paper and went to her sandbox to play.

"It would be wonderful to buy the horse for Sue," said Pam.

"Only," said Ricky glumly, "I haven't any money." He was not good at saving the nickels, dimes, and quarters that he earned. Instead, Ricky usually bought ice cream, a baseball, or something else he liked.

Pam was just the opposite. "I have some money saved up," she said. "So has Pete. Together we might have enough to buy the hobby horse. Anyway, we can bid on it and maybe we'll get it."

When she told Pete the plan, he was glad to help. The Hollister family always had fun together and also enjoyed helping others. For this reason people had come to call them the Happy Hollisters.

While Pam took the newspaper to her mother, Ricky told Holly their secret. "Promise you won't tell Sue," he said.

"Honest injun," his sister replied.

Ricky scratched his head. "But I think we ought to tell somebody."

Holly agreed that it was too good a secret not to whisper to some of their friends, so the two children skipped down the street to the home of Jeff and Ann Hunter. Dark-haired Jeff, who was eight, was standing on his front lawn. He was talking to a bigger boy who stood astride a bicycle.

"Yikes!" Ricky sighed. "There's Joey Brill." Joey

9

was Pete's age, but taller and heavier. He had played so many mean tricks on the Hollister children since they had moved to Shoreham that they avoided him whenever possible.

"Hi, Ricky! Hi, Holly!" Jeff called when he saw his friends. "Going to the big auction tomorrow at the haunted house?"

"You bet!" Ricky grinned.

"We're going to buy something special," Holly piped up.

"What?" Joey demanded.

"That's a secret," Holly giggled.

"You Hollister kids give me a pain," Joey grumbled. "Always a secret or a mystery or something. You think you're great, but you're not!"

Just then ten-year-old Ann Hunter ran from the side of the house. Ann was pretty, with lovely dimples and dark hair which hung in ringlets.

"Who has a secret?" she asked, laughing and looking from one to another.

"These Hollister kids say they have one, but they don't at all," Joey said.

"We do too!" Holly retorted, stamping her foot.

"Then what is it?" Joey teased.

"It's a horse!" Ricky blurted out.

"Oh, I know now! The hobbyhorse," Joey smirked. "I saw that in the auction-sale ad. Well, you're out of luck, because I'm going to buy the horse."

"Don't believe him," Ann said. "Joey will have to bid the same as anyone else, and the highest bidder will get it."

"Really? You'll see!" Joey said. He leaned over and yanked one of Holly's pigtails.

"Ouch!"

"Stop that!" Ricky shouted.

"Make me!" Joey retorted, and gave the boy a push which sent him sprawling on the grass.

At this moment the Hollisters' faithful collie came bounding along the street. Sensing trouble, he growled at Joey. At once the bully hopped onto his bicycle and sped off.

"I'm sorry Joey was here and made trouble for you," Ann said, putting an arm around Holly. Although Ann was a closer friend of Pam's, she was also very fond of Holly.

"It's not your fault," Holly said, but she added, "Do you suppose Joey'll get the hobbyhorse?"

"Everybody will have a chance," Ann said reassuringly. "Don't worry about it."

But Holly did worry, right up to the time of the auction the next morning. At quarter to ten the whole Hollister family set out in their station wagon, leaving Zip to guard the house and the garage, in which Domingo, their pet burro, had his stall.

Mr. Hollister drove through town and out to the countryside where the Stone farm was. He

11

parked, and the family walked across the lawn to the dilapidated house. Many other people were already there, milling about.

All the articles to be sold were scattered about the rickety old porch and on the grass. Standing on a low box in the middle of the porch was the auctioneer, Mr. Howe. He was stout and red-faced, and wore a felt hat pushed to the back of his head. He held a gavel in one hand. Every so often he would put the other into his pocket, pull out a big gold watch, and glance at it.

"Evidently Mr. Howe is going to start promptly at ten," Mrs. Hollister said with a chuckle as she looked over some of the antiques.

The children glanced about, too, but the hobby-horse which had been advertised was nowhere in sight.

"Maybe it's in the house," Ricky suggested. "Let's look!" he urged his brother and sisters.

He led the way inside the old house. How musty and damp it smelled!

"This is spooky," Ricky said, looking at the girls and pretending to shiver. Then he grinned. "Let's go upstairs."

The Hollister children climbed the squeaky steps, from which the carpeting had been removed. Arriving at the second floor, they scattered to the various rooms. Sue, a little afraid, stood near the stairway to wait for them.

12

Suddenly a boy dashed out of a hall closet nearby, yelling "Boo!" He bumped squarely into Sue, who lost her balance. With a cry, the little girl tumbled down the stairs!

CHAPTER 2

GOING—GOING—GONE!

Sue rolled head over heels down the stairway of the old farmhouse and landed at the bottom with a thump.

"Ow!" she wailed. "I'm hurted!"

Joey Brill, who had been the cause of Sue's tumble, raced past her and scooted from the house without stopping to help her up or say he was sorry for the accident.

Sue's cries brought her brothers and sisters from the second floor. And Mrs. Hollister hurried indoors to see what had happened. Fortunately Sue had only skinned her right knee and elbow. Mrs. Hollister said she would get the first-aid kit from the station wagon. When they heard of Joey's trick, all of them were indignant, and Pete whispered to Ricky that he was going to teach Joey a lesson.

"I'll help you," said Ricky.

As they started off, Holly joined them, saying she had overheard the plan. The three children threaded their way through the crowd to the place where Joey was now standing.

"You can't hurt my little sister and get away with it!" Pete cried angrily.

"I didn't do anything," Joey said, scowling. "She tripped and fell down the stairs."

"Joey, you pushed her!" Pete insisted.

"At least you ought to say you're sorry," Holly spoke up.

But Joey would not do this. He kept insisting it was an accident, and the Hollisters were willing to give Joey the benefit of the doubt.

"Well, don't do it again," Pete said as they started to move away.

"I will if I want to," Joey said and dug Pete in the ribs with his elbow as he passed by.

Pete spun around and punched Joey on the chest, as Mrs. Brill hurried toward them. "Here, here, stop fighting with my boy!" she cried out.

"He hit me first," Pete protested.

"Why don't you children run along," Mr. Brill said, "and quit bothering my son?"

"Well, of all the nerve!" Holly said as the three Hollisters walked back to where their parents were waiting for the auction to start. Sue, a bandage on her knee and elbow, had dried her tears and was smiling again. Holly started to tell her about Joey, but just then the auctioneer's gavel brought the crowd to attention.

"Everything from this house," the man shouted, "will be sold today. Bid high, bid low, but bid for these valuable articles."

Everyone pressed forward around the porch. Mr.

Howe reached down to the floor and lifted an old copper kettle to the table beside him.

"Here is a real antique," he said, banging on the side of the kettle with his gavel. "Who will start the bidding?"

"One dollar," came a voice from the crowd.

"Two dollars," said another.

"I'll bid three," Mr. Hollister cried out.

"Do I hear four dollars?" the auctioneer asked. "This is a real antique."

Somebody bid four dollars, and Mrs. Hollister whispered to her husband, "I'd love to have it to put beside our fireplace, John."

"Please get the kettle, Dad," Pam said. "It's beautiful."

"I could drum on it," Ricky put in.

"Five dollars!" Mr. Hollister called.

Mr. Howe banged his gavel and asked for a higher bid, but there was none. Then he said, "Going—going—gone—to that gentleman for five dollars."

"Yikes!" Ricky cried out, dashing forward to claim the prize and pay the five dollars. "Mother can make an awful lot of soup in this kettle!" Everybody laughed at the boy's remark.

The auction continued. Tables, chairs, and old lamps were put up and sold, but Mr. and Mrs. Hollister did not bid on any of them. Pete and Ricky, not particularly interested, had wandered off to look further for the hobbyhorse.

Presently Mr. Howe held up an old dinner bell. "How much am I bid for this?" he asked, shaking it a little. It made a deep, musical sound.

"Mother," said Holly, "that's just what you need to call the Happy Hollisters to dinner." The girl opened her hand and gazed at a twenty-five cent piece she held. "I think I'll bid for it," she added, tugging her mother's arm. Then in a loud voice, she exclaimed, "I bid twenty-five cents for the dinner bell."

The onlookers laughed because they knew the bell was worth much more.

"I have twenty-five cents," the auctioneer shouted. "Will somebody offer a dollar?"

But his audience was so amused by Holly that they did not raise the bid even one penny.

"Going—going—gone to the little girl for twenty-five cents," the man said, smiling as Holly went forward to get the bell.

As she retreated into the crowd, Holly passed close to Joey Brill. "You think you're real tricky, don't you, buying that bell so cheap," he said.

Holly held her head high and tossed her pigtails but did not reply. When she returned to her family, Pete and Ricky were back. All the children crowded around to look at the dinner bell.

"Let's see it for a second," Ricky said, and gave the bell a couple of rings.

"Quiet!" Pam warned him. "The auction is going on again."

"We still can't find the hobbyhorse that was in the ad," Pete said. "We've been looking all around for it."

Ricky frowned, "Do you suppose Joey bought it before the sale started?"

"That wouldn't be fair," said Pam. "Come on, let's look around again. Maybe it's hidden under something."

The five children ambled around the fringe of the crowd, examining the various things that were left for sale. Several pieces of wicker furniture were piled on top of one another. Pete set them on the grass one by one in order to make sure the hobbyhorse was not hidden beneath them.

"Maybe the horse galloped away," Sue guessed.

"It *has* to be somewhere around here," Ricky exclaimed impatiently.

"It could have been a misprint in the newspaper," Pete suggested. He was about to say they might as well give up when Pam noticed a big pile of stair carpeting which lay on the ground. She ran over to it.

"Oh, look!" Pam shouted, tugging at the faded heap of material. "Something's underneath this."

Ricky and Pete pushed the carpet aside. The head of a wooden hobbyhorse appeared.

"Crickets!" Pete exclaimed. "Somebody was trying to hide this."

As he glanced around Pete caught sight of Joey Brill. "I'll bet he did it."

The children quickly uncovered the rest of the old

"I'll bet Joey was trying to hide this."

hobbyhorse. It was attached to rockers and was about four feet long. The saddle on the horse's back was two and a half feet from the ground.

"He's swell," Ricky declared, noticing that the toy was still in good condition.

The horse's body was painted white with black splotches of various sizes. A black horsehair mane and tail looked surprisingly real.

"But the pony has measles," said Sue, looking at the black spots in alarm. "Oh, the poor sick hobbyhorse!"

"Those aren't measle spots," Pam laughed. "They show what kind of horse he is."

"Then what kind is he?" Sue challenged her.

"I don't know," Pam admitted.

"I'm going to find out," Sue declared. She hurried back to her father and described the hobbyhorse to him in great detail.

"That's probably an imitation appaloosa horse," Mr. Hollister told her. "I'd have to see it to be sure."

"Thank you, Daddy." Sue dashed back to the other children. "It's a applesauce horse," she announced. "I want to take a ride."

Pam thought it best if one of the larger children got on first to be sure the hobbyhorse was safe. It was plenty big enough for a seven-year-old, so Ricky was elected. He put his left foot in the stirrup and swung himself onto the pony's back.

"Wow, this is a regular western saddle!" the boy

said gleefully and started to rock on the horse. "Yippee! Ride 'em cowboy!" he exclaimed.

"May I have a turn?" Holly asked.

"Of course," Pam said. "But give Ricky time to have a good ride."

"I want a ride!" came the demanding voice of Joey Brill. He strode over to the hobbyhorse and stood directly in front of it. "Come on, you've ridden long enough, Ricky. It's my turn."

"It's not," Ricky said, making the hobbyhorse go faster and faster.

"Let Ricky alone," Pete warned the bully. "You come last after all of us."

"Oh, is that so!" Joey said menacingly. "As soon as your brother is finished I'm going to have a ride." Joey took a step closer to the hobbyhorse.

"Get out of the way!" Ricky ordered. "The horse might bite you!"

"You'd better not try——ow!" Joey let out a scream as the horse's hoofs banged him in the shin. Joey doubled up, grabbed his leg with both hands, and danced around in pain.

"I'm sorry, but I told you not to get too close!" Ricky said, noting that Joey was not really hurt. But Joey put up such a howl that the auction was stopped for a moment and everybody turned to find out what had happened.

"He made the horse kick me," the bully wailed, looking at the people. "I wanted a ride and he wouldn't give me one!" Ignoring this, Ricky leaped off the horse so that Sue might have a turn. But before the little girl could get on, the auctioneer walked over to them.

"This is a valuable antique," he said. "If you children fight over it, the horse may get broken. Leave it alone." Then he added, "I'll settle this once and for all."

Mr. Howe picked up the horse and carried it to the auction table. The Hollister children followed, and went to stand beside their parents.

"What am I bid for this splendid old hobby-horse?" Mr. Howe shouted.

Pam quickly turned to her mother and whispered, "Pete and I have ten dollars between us. We'd like to buy the hobbyhorse for Sue."

"That's wonderful," Mrs. Hollister replied. "Put in a low bid!"

"Do I hear an offer?" the auctioneer asked.

"Two dollars!" Joey Brill called out, raising his hand high and waving it for attention.

"Three!" Pam said.

Several other people joined in the bidding. It reached eight dollars. Then Joey cried loudly, "I'll bid nine for the hobbyhorse."

"Oh, dear," Pam whispered to Pete. "We have only ten dollars. Shall we bid it all?"

"Sure, go ahead!"

"Ten dollars!" Pam raised her voice.

There was silence for a moment. Joey Brill glared

at the Hollisters. Suddenly he whispered to his parents, then with a smirk he shouted:

"Eleven dollars!"

"What are we going to do now?" Pam said sadly. She turned to her father. "Daddy, do you suppose——"

Before she had time to finish what she wanted to say the auctioneer bellowed, "I have eleven dollars! Do I hear another bid? Going, going——"

CHAPTER 3

A LUCKY TUMBLE

THE auctioneer held his gavel high in the air. He was about to bring it down, indicating a final sale, when Pete Hollister cried out, "Twelve dollars!"

"What was that?" Mr. Howe asked.

As Pete repeated his bid, Joey Brill set up a cry of protest. "I already won the hobbyhorse!" he complained. "You can't do this!"

"The bid was not closed," Mr. Howe said in annoyance. "I have twelve dollars—do I hear a higher bid? If not—going, going, gone! To Pete Hollister!" The auctioneer brought his gavel down with a bang.

"It's not fair!" Joey Brill shouted, but Mr. Howe paid no attention to him.

Pete and Ricky went forward to pay the money, then returned with the hobbyhorse. Winking at his father, Pete said, "Thanks a lot for the two extra dollars, Dad. I'll earn it."

"You can do that working at the Trading Post," Mr. Hollister said, smiling. Pete often helped his father after school and on Saturdays to earn money.

"And now," said Pam, turning Sue's dimpled

face toward her own, "you have a hobbyhorse to ride on, Sue."

"You mean this is for me?" the little girl cried with delight. "You and Pete buyed it for me?" They nodded, and she reached up to kiss them both. With a giggle, Sue added, "Do you think our burro Domingo will like to play with the new hobbyhorse?"

"Of course," Pam laughed. "They'll be good friends."

By now Joey and his parents had started to walk toward their parked car. As the mean boy went past Pete, he hissed in his ear, "I'll get you for this!"

Then, without warning, the bully bent down, picked up the dinner bell, and flung it at the copper kettle.

Clang! What a noise it made! The auctioneer stopped his work and everyone turned to look. Suddenly the Hollisters realized they were being blamed for the disturbance.

Pete was angry. He started after Joey, but before he could reach the bully, Joey had dashed to the Brills' car and locked himself in. A few seconds later his parents arrived and the family rode off, with Joey making faces at Pete.

Pam had run up to her brother. "Well, I'm glad Joey's out of the way," she said with a sigh. "He's too old for a hobbyhorse, anyway."

"Joey just didn't want us to have it," Pete declared. "But we fooled him, thanks to Dad."

As the auction proceeded, Holly and Sue took turns riding the hobbyhorse. Tiring of this, after awhile, Holly said to her little sister, "Let's see what's behind the house."

Taking Sue's hand, she walked with her around the side of the building. The back yard was full of high weeds, in the middle of which stood an old apple tree. Some of its gnarled branches reached down to the ground.

"Oh, look, there's a rope hanging from one of the limbs," Holly said. "Maybe we can swing on it."

"Let's try," Sue said happily, grasping the rope. It dangled several feet off the ground.

"Hold onto it and I'll push you," said Holly. Sue grabbed hold of the rope more tightly.

"This is fun!" she squealed as she swung to and fro. When Sue had had enough of this, she dropped to the ground.

Holly started to climb up the tree trunk. "I'm going to shin down the rope," she said. By pulling herself up from one branch to another, she finally reached the one to which the rope was tied. It was about ten feet from the ground.

"I'll make believe I'm a fireman and the rope is my fire pole," Holly called to Sue. "When I slide down it, you make a noise like a fire bell. Here I come!" Holly shouted.

"*Clang! Clang! Clang!*" Sue cried in reply.

Suddenly there was a ripping sound. One of the strands of the old rope had broken. Then *snap*,

26

another came apart. Holly looked up fearfully. The whole rope was parting just above her head!

"Help! Help!" she called out. "I'm going to fall!" Sue, frightened, did not know what to do.

"Hold on! I'll catch you!" came a boy's voice. Across the yard raced a youth about sixteen years old, wearing a white shirt and dark trousers. He dropped a small suitcase he was carrying.

As the last strand of rope broke, the boy reached the apple tree. He held out his arms and Holly tumbled into them. The force of the impact sent them both to the ground, but unhurt.

"*Whew!*" he whistled, helping Holly and himself up. "That was close!"

"It sure was!" Holly grinned. "Thank you for saving me. I didn't know the rope was rotten."

"Naughty rope!" said Sue, shaking her fist at the piece which lay on the ground.

Holly's cries for help had brought the rest of her family, who saw the rescue. Turning to the strange boy, Mrs. Hollister thanked him for saving Holly from a bad fall.

"I was glad to help," he replied, smiling. "When I was a kid I used to play here myself."

"Did you swing on this tree?" asked Sue.

"Yes I did and I'll bet this is part of the old rope swing," the youth replied.

The Hollisters introduced themselves. In turn, he said he was Graham Stone, grandson of old Mr. Stone, who had died a month before.

"Help! Help!" Holly cried.

"We're sorry about your grandfather's death," said Mrs. Hollister.

"I am, too," said Graham soberly. "Grandpa was a very kind old man, but people didn't understand him. I hadn't seen him since I was Ricky's age."

"Why is that?" asked Ricky curiously.

"S-s-ssh!" said Pam, remembering that Graham was an orphan and now, without his grandfather, probably had no relatives to love him.

Graham smiled at Pam, having overheard. "I don't mind explaining," he said. Then he told them that he had lived far down south since he was seven years old. Because his parents had been poor, they had never been able to afford a trip up to Shoreham. And old Mr. Stone had not been strong enough to travel south. Two years before, when he was fourteen, Graham had lost his parents.

"After this happened," he continued, "Grandpa offered me a home here at the farm. My parents didn't leave me any money, but I also knew that Grandpa could barely afford to take care of himself. So I got a job in my home town where I received room and board, plus some spending money."

"That was a brave thing to do, Graham," Mrs. Hollister exclaimed with admiration.

The youth looked at the ground modestly. "There was nothing else I could do," he said finally. "I wanted to finish high school and I still have two more years to go. Somehow—somewhere, I'll have to save enough money to go to college. I want to be a veterinarian."

"You mean an animal doctor?" Pete asked.

"That's right," said Graham.

"You'll get lots of money from this auction sale, Graham," said Pete reassuringly. "You can use it to go to college."

"The auction was a big surprise to me," Graham replied seriously. He explained that he had not known of his grandfather's death until that very morning, when he arrived in town.

"Oh, I'm so sorry," said Mrs. Hollister instantly.

Graham said that five weeks before he had received a letter from old Mr. Stone saying he was not well. Worried, Graham had taken all his savings from the bank when his school term had finished. Then he had made the journey to Shoreham and learned the sad news.

"Why didn't someone write you?" asked Ricky.

"Probably because no one could find my address," Graham guessed. Then he said that his grandfather had been eccentric. For one thing, he never saved a bit of paper or any letters. There would have been no way to trace Graham had anyone tried.

"Did you ever ride the applesauce horse when you visited here?" Sue interrupted. Graham looked puzzled until Mr. Hollister explained that she meant the appaloosa hobbyhorse.

"Oh, sure," he nodded. "I rode it many times.

Grandpa made it and modeled the hobbyhorse after a real appaloosa horse he had once seen."

"We bought it today," said Holly. "Does he have a special name?"

"I think I just called him Horsie when I was young," Graham laughed.

The more he talked, the better the Hollister children liked the boy. Ricky decided it would be all right to ask him a certain question.

"Is this farmhouse really haunted?" he said.

"Of course not," replied Graham, amused. He said his grandfather had been an inventor of gadgets and used to enjoy playing tricks on his guests with them.

"Grandpa could make the shutters bang and the stairs squeak," the boy explained, chuckling. "He even had a mechanical owl in the attic which would hoot when anybody opened the door."

The Hollisters laughed, and Ricky asked if any of the gadgets were still here.

"I guess not, but we can look around," Graham offered. "We'll go to the barn first."

Mrs. Hollister wanted to go back to the auction and bid on a few pieces of glassware. Graham said he would stay with the children.

He led them through the weeds toward an old red barn which was built against the side of a hill. Holly, Ricky, and Sue skipped on ahead.

"This is where I had the most fun of all," Graham told Pam and Pete, smiling and pointing to the barn. "There's something hidden in there that I know you'll like."

"What is it?" they both asked.

"You'll see."

The doors of the old barn stood open, showing stalls where horses and cows once had been kept. The visitors went inside.

"Where is the big secret?" Pam asked, looking all around her and seeing nothing unusual.

"On the second floor," Graham said, "if it's still there." He started to climb the stairs to the loft. "It's a lot older than I am," he hinted, as the Hollisters followed close behind.

When they reached the barn loft, whose rear door opened onto the hillside, several swallows flitted through the broken window panes.

Pointing to a corner, Graham said, "I think it's right behind those old bales of hay. Last time I was here I covered it up with straw."

As they walked toward a corner where the bales were piled up, Ricky nearly stepped into a hole in the rotted floor. He caught himself just in time.

Graham tossed back several handfuls of straw. "Ah, just as I left it!" he cried.

"An old jalopy!" Ricky exclaimed. "Say, this is keen!"

"I'll bet it's older than Daddy!" Pam said with a chuckle. "Look at that funny steering wheel!"

"And the skinny tires," Holly giggled.

"Does the car still run?" Pete asked Graham.

"I doubt it. The only thing that used to work on it was this old horn." Graham pressed it.

Ooga! Ooga! It was a sorrowful sound and made the children laugh.

"Say, is this the treasure people say is hidden on the farm?" Ricky asked.

"Oh, no," Graham said, laughing. Then he added, "The treasure's a mystery to me, too. Come on. We'd better go back to the house."

But the children would not go until each one had seated himself in the driver's seat of the car and blown the horn several times. Ricky was first and also the last one to have a turn.

As he stepped down, he bumped against the steering wheel. *Crack!* The old column had rusted through and the wheel fell to the floor of the car.

"Now you've done it!" Holly cried.

"Gee, I'm sorry," Ricky said. "I'll fix it for you, Graham."

"It's not worth fixing," the boy reassured him. "Don't worry! But now I think I hear your parents whistling for you. We'd better go."

They left the barn and raced to tell Mr. and Mrs. Hollister of the wonderful car.

Graham smiled. "If this farm comes to me as Grandpa's only relative, I'll let you boys have the old jalopy."

"That'll be great!" cried Pete enthusiastically.

Pam again asked what Graham thought the treasure might be which people talked about. The boy shook his head, declaring he did not know.

"The only clue I have to any treasure," he said, "is in my last letter from my grandfather. The money from the auction sale and from selling the farm later on will probably go to pay off Grandpa's debts. He owed many people money."

Graham put his hand into a pocket and pulled out a letter. Unfolding it, he showed one paragraph to Mr. Hollister.

"It is very blurry," he explained.

"The only words I can make out," Mr. Hollister said, "are 'Mystery boy, this is the only thing of value I can leave you.'"

"Did he call you 'mystery boy'?" Ricky wanted to know.

"Not that I know of," Graham remarked. "Anyway, Grandpa never used that name to my face. I really don't know what he meant."

"Then maybe there's some other kind of mystery boy," Pam remarked. "Could it be the nickname for one of your grandfather's secret inventions?"

Graham did not know this either.

"Maybe there's a clue in the house," Holly suggested.

"Perhaps there is!" said Graham, brightening.

"Then let's search the house for the treasure!" Ricky urged, and dashed toward the rear door.

CHAPTER 4

TREASURE BOX

THE IDEA of hunting for a treasure in the old farmhouse had not occurred to Graham Stone. Now he was intrigued by the idea.

"I wouldn't know where to look, though," he said, following the Hollister children inside the house.

"Things are sometimes hidden behind loose stones in a fireplace," Pete suggested.

They examined every inch of the stonework, and Graham tapped the mantel and around the wide boards in front of the stone hearth.

Ricky clambered into the gloomy room.

"No secret sliding boards here," he said finally.

Ricky had ventured deep into the fireplace and peered up the chimney. When he showed his face again it was full of soot.

"Look at you!" Pam said, taking her handkerchief and wiping her brother's face.

"If I'm going to be a real detective," Ricky said in protest, "I have to get dirty."

Next they began to search through cupboards and closets. Far back on one of the pantry shelves Holly discovered a broken cup with a penny in it and gleefully called out that she had found a treasure. When the others rushed up to see what it was, the pigtailed girl displayed an Indian-head penny.

"That's an antique," Graham said, laughing. "Come on. Let's look further."

After the first floor of the farmhouse had been thoroughly covered, the children clomped up the front stairway, down which Sue had tumbled. The closets on the second floor were as empty as Mother Hubbard's cupboard. And there were no secret openings in the floor. As they stood in a back bedroom, Graham pointed to a trap door in the ceiling.

"How do you get up there?" Ricky asked. "There isn't any ladder."

"Maybe you could stand on my shoulders," Graham suggested, "and push the trap door open."

Ricky did this and clambered into the gloomy

room which had a tiny window covered with dust.

"Yikes! What cobwebs!" he called down to the others.

"Is there anything else up there?" Pete asked him.

"Wait a minute. I'll see," his brother replied.

The children below could hear Ricky walking about above their heads. Suddenly they heard him cry out, "I've found it! I've found the treasure!"

"What is it?" they cried out together.

"An old tin box!" Ricky said, peering down through the opening.

In his hands he held a rusty box. Its lid was fastened shut by a lock. Ricky shook the box.

"It sounds as if it's full of coins," he said. "Help me down, please, Graham."

As Ricky wiggled through the opening, Graham stood beneath him and guided the boy's feet to his shoulders. Then Ricky jumped to the floor clutching the box.

"I found it under the eaves," he said, handing the box to Graham. "Hurry, let's open it and find out what the treasure is!"

The older boy tried to open the old lock on the box. It would not budge.

"We'll find a hammer and break it," Graham said enthusiastically. He hurried down the stairs with the five Hollister children trailing behind him.

Meeting Mr. and Mrs. Hollister on the front porch, he said, "Ricky found the treasure. Look!"

"Wonderful," said Mrs. Hollister. "How are you going to get the lock off?"

"Break it, I guess," Graham replied. "We haven't a key."

Ricky, meanwhile, had been rummaging around in one pocket. Presently he pulled out a long nail. "Maybe you can twist the lock off with this," he said.

Graham took the nail and pushed it through the hasp. Then with a strong, quick twist, he snapped the lock. As the children watched breathlessly, Graham lifted the lid of the box.

"Buttons!" the children moaned.

The box was full of buttons of all kinds and description. Big ones, little ones, copper ones, wooden ones.

"My grandmother's collection, no doubt," Graham said. "And I suppose it ought to go into the auction. We'll take it downstairs."

"I'd love to have it," Pam said.

Pete thought they ought to see first if any treasure were hidden deep inside. Graham dumped the contents of the box on the floor. Nothing but buttons lay in the heap. The boy put them back and led the way to the porch.

By this time the auction was over and people were leaving. Graham explained to the auctioneer about finding the buttons and asked what they should do about it. Pam Hollister would like to have them.

Mr. Howe smiled. "Tell you what. Suppose we

39

have a private auction. If you haven't any money, bid with anything you have."

Sue giggled. "I bid one stick of gum for the buttons," she said, pulling it from her pocket.

Pete and Ricky did not want the box so they kept still, but Holly said, "One lollypop."

Poor Pam! She could not think of anything she had with her that the auctioneer would consider. But there was just a chance of one item—

"I'll bid a card with a fortune on it," she said timidly, putting her hand into a pocket. "I got it in a weight telling machine. It's a good fortune, though."

Mr. Howe roared with laughter. Then he said, "Going, going, gone! To the little girl with the good fortune." As Pam handed him the card, he added, "I can use a little good luck, so I'll take this card myself and put twenty-five cents in the day's receipts." He did this and then wrote the sale down in a book.

"Did you make lots of money for Graham?" Holly asked him.

"Graham?" the auctioneer said. "This sale was for old Mr. Stone's estate."

The youth explained who he was and that he had just arrived in Shoreham. Mr. Howe, who lived at a distance, knew nothing about Mr. Stone's will and so could not tell Graham.

The boy said, "I'm going to town to find Grandfather's lawyer or someone who will know."

Mr. Howe offered to take him. "I'll be going in a few minutes," he said.

While he was packing up, the children went with Graham to where Mr. and Mrs. Hollister were waiting. Pam showed her mother the box of buttons.

"Why many of these are very old and interesting," Mrs. Hollister said. "Some of them were worn on Civil War uniforms. They shouldn't be played with. Pam, they'd make lovely earrings."

"Then I got a real bargain," her daughter said, laughing.

"Indeed you did."

While they were waiting for the auctioneer to drive Graham to town, Pete asked the boy to tell them more about himself.

"I work on a farm where they raise horses," the boy said.

"That must be fun," Pam remarked.

"It is," Graham said. "We raise appaloosas—the same kind as that hobbyhorse you bought. They're very smart animals, and we train them for circus work."

"You're a horse trainer?" Pete asked in amazement.

"Well, sort of," came the reply. "I like to ride, especially appaloosas. They're fine horses."

"How did the poor things get the measles?" Sue said suddenly.

Graham and the others laughed. He said that the spotted appaloosas were used in China in ancient days.

"But our hobbyhorse doesn't have slanted eyes like Chinese people," Holly said, cocking her head.

Her funny remark made everyone laugh again. Then Graham began his story about the history of the lovely horses.

"The ancient Chinese called them the Heavenly Horses," he went on. "And they were the favorites of the emperor."

"How did they happen to come to America?" Pam wanted to know.

Graham said that the appaloosa had been brought first to Mexico by the Spanish. This was years before the real explorations began. "The Indians bred them," he said, "and became fond of the appaloosas because of their intelligence and endurance. They are very speedy, yet gentle." Graham explained that the Nez Percé tribe of Idaho had bred hundreds of them.

"How interesting!" Mrs. Hollister remarked. "Where is the horse farm on which you work, Graham?"

The boy told them that it was a long way off down south where there were many horse farms. "And I'll have to go back there soon," he said. "I work for a very nice man. He depends on me, so I don't want to be away too long."

By this time the auctioneer was ready to leave.

He was already in his car and bringing it down the driveway of the farmhouse. Graham started to say good-by to the Hollisters.

After a few whispered words to her husband, Mrs. Hollister said to him, "We'd be very happy to have you come to supper and stay overnight with us, Graham."

"Thank you, Mrs. Hollister, I'd like to. After I attend to some business in town, I'll come."

Mrs. Hollister gave Graham directions. Then he stepped into Mr. Howe's car and waved, "See you all later."

The Hollisters called good-by, then went to their station wagon and piled in. Arriving at their home, Mr. Hollister carried the rocking horse in. The boys followed with articles from the auction. They set all of them in the living room. Pam and Holly hurried in with the box of buttons.

"Come on," Pam said to her sister. "We'll use Daddy's workbench to make some earrings." The two girls hurried to the basement, where Pam kept a special kit for making jewelry which she had received from Mrs. Ruth Thomas, a cousin of Mrs. Hollister's.

Ricky and Sue, meanwhile, had opened the garage door to play with their little black burro. Ricky led Domingo outside, lifted Sue to the animal's back, and paraded around the yard with them several times. Sue began to rock back and forth, to see if Domingo would behave like the rocking horse.

"Oh, dear, I guess you're not an applesauce pony," the little girl said with a sigh.

"I know how we can make him one," Ricky replied with a gleam in his eyes.

"How?"

Ricky lifted his sister off the burro and whispered something in her ear.

"Oh, let's do it," Sue said, jumping up and down.

The children led Domingo back into the garage and closed the doors. Then Ricky reached up for a can of whitewash on a shelf. As he pried open the lid he said, "Golly, we haven't any paintbrush!"

"We can use a stick," Sue replied, picking one up from the floor.

"Sure, that'll do."

While all this was going on, Domingo stood in his stall, twitching his ears and looking back over his shoulder at the two children, as if to say, "What's going on here?"

"Now we're ready to paint you, Domingo, to make you an applesauce horse," Sue giggled.

Ricky put the stick into the whitewash and began to daub some blotches on the burro's flank. Domingo did not like this. Nervously he stepped from side to side, trying to avoid the stick.

"Whoa, Domingo! Hold still so we can paint some spots on you!" Ricky commanded.

But the more Ricky painted him, the more annoyed the burro became. Finally the animal gave a little kick. His hoofs hit the can of whitewash and it flew high into the air.

"Look out, Ricky!" Sue cried.

But her brother could not get out of the way in time. The paint bucket landed upside down on top of his head!

"*Yikes!*" Ricky cried.

CHAPTER 5

A BIG DISCOVERY

"Yikes!" Ricky cried, quickly closing his eyes tight.

He pulled the bucket off his head and threw it on the floor. But already the whitewash had run through his hair, down his face and was dripping onto his clothes. Ricky put up his hands to wipe it off, then in disgust shook the whitewash from his fingertips.

Sue did not realize how uncomfortable he was. She began to giggle. "Oh, Ricky, you look so funny!"

Her brother did not think it was laughable. "How can I wipe this off when I can't open my eyes?" he cried. "Sue, get me a towel."

At this moment Domingo gave a loud *Ee-aw.*

"I guess our burro didn't want to be made into a horse," Sue said as she skipped toward the house. "Mother!" she called. "Come look at Ricky and bring a towel to wipe off his applesauce!"

Mrs. Hollister, who was in the kitchen preparing lunch, thought Sue meant real applesauce. She did not hurry as she tore two paper towels off the holder.

But when she came outside and saw Ricky, who was standing in the doorway of the garage, she exclaimed in dismay.

"Goodness gracious! Oh dear me! What have you done?"

"We were painting Domingo," Sue exclaimed. "And he kicked the bucket way up high. And it came down whoops on Ricky."

Her mother ran toward Ricky. She wiped his face and head carefully with the towels so he dared open his eyes. Then she covered his head with a large cloth she had asked Sue to bring from the garage.

"Stay here until I come back," she told him. "I'll have to wash your hair."

Mrs. Hollister disappeared into the house. In a few moments she returned with a bucket of sudsy water and a stiff brush. Ricky removed his shirt and leaned over. She scrubbed his whitened hair until it was red again.

By this time Sue had gone to tell the other children and they came running. She led them into the garage to look at Domingo. What a sight he was!

"Oh you poor thing!" Pam cried sympathetically.

Pete laughed. "I don't blame you for kicking at the bucket," he told the burro. "Pam, Holly and I will clean you up."

"You can use this pail," Mrs. Hollister said. "I've finished with it."

All the whitewash had been removed from Ricky

48

but he was sopping wet with soapy water. "Now go in and take a shower," his mother said.

Pete took the pail and went for some more soap and water. Returning, he said, "Say, Domingo does look like a spotted appaloosa." He went to work with the brush.

"*Ee-aw! Ee-aw!*" the burro kept braying as Pete washed down his flanks. Finally they were clean and unspotted. Domingo nuzzled the boy as if in thanks, then lay down to rest.

Ricky was unusually quiet during lunch and all afternoon, but the prospect of Graham's visiting them finally made him happy again.

"I hope he comes in time for supper," Pam said as she and Holly set the table. But when the food was ready and Graham had not arrived, Mrs. Hollister suggested that the family sit down to eat.

"We can reheat Graham's dinner if he comes," she said.

As Pete held his mother's chair out for her to be seated, Pam slipped a little package in front of her plate.

"Why, what's this?" asked Mrs. Hollister. The older girls smiled as she opened it and exclaimed, "Oh, beautiful earrings!"

"Holly helped me make them from the old buttons this afternoon," Pam explained.

"Thank you both!" their mother said, blowing each girl a kiss. She at once clipped the tiny brass eagles to her ears.

During the meal the children kept glancing toward the front door, hoping to see Graham standing there. But he did not appear.

Before Mrs. Hollister served dessert, she said to her husband, "John, why don't you telephone the auctioneer and find out if he knows where Graham went. Perhaps he forgot our name and address. We could call him, if he's still at the lawyer's."

Agreeing, Mr. Hollister walked to the telephone in the hall. After a short conversation with Mr. Howe, he put down the receiver and returned to his family.

"Mr. Howe hasn't any idea where Graham went," he reported. "He left him on a corner in downtown Shoreham. I suppose I could call up various lawyers and check to see which one is handling Mr. Stone's estate."

"Never mind," said Mrs. Hollister. "Most offices will be closed now anyway. Maybe Graham will still come here."

After a delicious dessert of frozen éclairs, Pam and Holly cleared the table. Meanwhile, Pete, Ricky, and Sue played with the hobbyhorse in the living room.

"We ought to oil it, don't you think?" Pete said. "Then it'll rock smoother."

Ricky agreed. Mr. Hollister told them to put some newspapers under the hobbyhorse while they oiled it. While Pete did this, Ricky went to the cellar for a can of oil.

The work began. Since Sue could not ride while

her brothers were oiling the horse, she began to inspect the toy more closely. Presently Sue lifted his mane. Underneath it a small oblong brass plate was tacked on. It was greenish with age, but Sue thought there were words on the plate.

"Look!" she exclaimed.

Her brothers stopped their work and followed Sue's pointing finger. Mr. Hollister, too, came to inspect the plate.

"This will have to be cleaned off before we can read it," he said.

"I'll get some sandpaper," Ricky offered and hurried off again to the cellar.

In the meantime, Sue asked what her father thought the metal piece said. "I believe it's the hobbyhorse's name," Mr. Hollister replied.

Pam and Holly had finished helping their mother and now came to watch what was going on.

Ricky arrived with the sandpaper and began using it on the name plate. "It's coming!" he announced.

"Can you read the name yet?" Holly asked excitedly.

"No, just a few of the letters," her brother answered.

Pete leaned over. He could dimly make out an *m*, a *t*, and a *b* cut into the metal plate. Taking the sandpaper from Ricky, he scraped a little harder.

"There, I see it now," Pete said. "Why—the name is Mystery Boy!"

"Mystery Boy?" Pam repeated in amazement.

"That's what Mr. Stone wrote in the letter to Graham when he said it was all he could leave him."

"You're right," Pete said. "Do you suppose Mr. Stone was talking about this hobbyhorse?"

"I'll bet he was," Pam replied. "Maybe there's a valuable secret connected with this rocking horse."

"I don't see how there could be," Ricky said, looking the animal over. "It's just an old wooden horse."

"Maybe the secret is in the name Mystery Boy," Holly mused. "Oh, if Graham would only come, maybe he could solve the whole mystery."

"But he didn't know the hobbyhorse had a name," Pete reminded her. "Also Graham didn't seem to think it was valuable or he would have felt bad because we bought it."

"You mean his grandfather didn't tell him that he was to inherit the horse some day?" said Holly. Pete nodded and the girl added, "Just the same, I wish he'd come."

Mrs. Hollister walked into the living room and heard the story. She suggested that old Mr. Stone must have put the name plate on the horse after Graham and his parents moved away. "And evidently he never told them. It's a real secret."

Mr. Hollister thought so too. Then he said how about all of them going outdoors a while before bedtime. They could watch for Graham.

For the rest of the evening the children played

52

on the front lawn. But when bedtime rolled around, Graham had not appeared.

"I hope nothing has happened to him," Pam said, worried.

"Graham should have phoned us if he wasn't coming," Pete said.

"Perhaps something happened that made him return to his home in the South in a hurry," Mrs. Hollister said. "I'm sure we'll hear from Graham when he has a chance to write, if that is the case. Just be patient, children."

Usually she did not have any trouble getting the younger children to bed. But this evening they were so excited about the day's events and the new rocking horse that they did not want to go upstairs. Each one begged for a last ride on Mystery Boy.

Sue, who had had the first ride, disappeared for a couple of minutes. Now she returned. The small girl was carrying the family cat, White Nose, and her five kittens.

"Look at me!" Sue giggled. "I'm covered with cats!"

The mother cat was under the little girl's left arm. Two of the kittens were cradled in her right elbow. Another was on her left shoulder, a fourth on her right shoulder and the fifth on the top of her head.

Everyone laughed, and Pam asked, "What are you going to do with them?"

"Give them all a ride on Mystery Boy," Sue replied.

The kittens miaowed and jumped to the floor. Sue picked them up and set them up on the hobby-horse's back.

"Tutti-Frutti," she scolded, "sit still!"

What a job it was to keep all the cats balanced at the same time! Midnight, Snowball, Smoky, and Cuddly were set behind Tutti-Frutti and White Nose was last. She slipped off once and clung to the horse's tail. Sue lifted her back on.

When the cats were finally in place, Sue started the horse rocking. Back and forth it went. The cats swayed, looking worried. Then White Nose let out a loud miaow, as if to tell her babies they had had enough. Instantly she and the kittens jumped off the horse together.

"I'll tend to the cats," Mr. Hollister said. "And now to bed. Ricky, Holly, and Sue first. The last one of you upstairs is a mud turtle!"

The three children giggled and scrambled up the stairs as fast as they could. Ricky was first but slipped on one of the steps and Holly got ahead of him. Then he tripped again, and Sue scooted past her brother.

"Ricky is *the* mud turtle!" she chanted.

"Well, I guess this just isn't my day," the boy said, grinning, and the three children prepared for bed.

Some time later the Hollister home became quiet

with everyone asleep. The kittens were in the cellar but Zip was left to wander around the house as a watchdog and sleep wherever he pleased.

In the middle of the night Holly was suddenly awakened by hearing Zip whine. Then the other children sat up in their beds as the dog began to bark.

"I think someone's trying to break into our house," Pam said anxiously to Holly, who roomed with her.

Out in the hall came Pete's voice. "Come on, Dad, let's go see what's bothering Zip."

All the children bounded out of their beds.

CHAPTER 6

FIRE-ENGINE TROUBLE

TIPTOEING down the dimly lit stairway after Mr. Hollister, Pete listened intently. Zip continued to whine, and this was accompanied by a squeaking sound.

Pam, at Pete's heels, whispered, "What can it be?"

Pete had to admit he could not figure out the sound. If there were a burglar in the house, Zip would have tackled him by now. As for the whining, the collie did this only when he was worried.

Before Mr. Hollister reached the last step, the entire family except Sue was on the staircase behind him. He switched on the living room light.

What a strange sight they saw! Zip was crouched on the floor gazing at the empty rocking horse, which was moving back and forth.

"Zingo! It's magic!" Ricky cried out as they all crowded around the toy.

"What is making it rock?" Pam asked.

"Somebody must have set it in motion," Mr. Hollister replied.

"Perhaps a strange person *is* in the house," the children's mother spoke up, glancing suspiciously around at the corners.

"I'll make a search," her husband announced. "You all stay here. Come on, Zip!"

He and the faithful collie searched through the first-floor rooms and then went into the cellar. Returning to the living room, Mr. Hollister said, "No one around."

Suddenly Holly asked, "Do you suppose Joey Brill came in here to get our hobbyhorse and Zip scared him away?"

Her father did not think so. "It's three o'clock in the morning," he remarked, glancing at his wrist watch. "Joey wouldn't be out at this hour."

"Then who started the hobbyhorse moving?" Holly persisted.

"I believe Zip nudged it with his nose," Mrs. Hollister said. "But see how the horse is still rocking."

"There must be some kind of machinery inside to keep it going," Pete guessed. "Otherwise it would have stopped long ago."

"Let's take the horse apart and see," Ricky urged.

Mr. Hollister said they all had better return to bed. "You can examine the hobbyhorse tomorrow after church," he added. "Upstairs, everybody!"

As the family climbed the steps, Pete said, "It's a shame we can't tell Graham about this."

"Yes it is," his father agreed.

After returning from church the next day, the Hollisters sat down to dinner. Talk at once turned to the hobbyhorse.

"Are we going to 'zamine him this afternoon?"

Sue asked as she ate her chocolate pudding topped with whipped cream.

"That's what Pete and I plan to do," Ricky said importantly. "Dad, will you help us?"

Mr. Hollister said he would be happy to. When the meal was over, his sons helped him carry the hobbyhorse down the cellar stairs. They laid the wooden animal on the work bench, then examined it carefully to see where it came apart.

The girls wanted to watch, too, but their father said it would be too crowded in his workroom for so many people. If they found anything interesting inside the horse, he would call them.

The three sisters went outdoors. Idly Holly picked up a croquet mallet and began to hit balls. She tapped one so hard that it rolled along the driveway and across the sidewalk. As she ran to get it, Holly saw a bus drive past. Glancing inside it, she gasped.

Graham Stone was a passenger! He did not see her, as he was looking straight ahead.

Picking up the croquet ball, Holly raced back to tell Pam and Sue.

"Are you sure it was Graham?" Pam asked.

When Holly insisted it was, the three girls ran into the house to inform their mother.

"We must find him!" Pam urged. "Mother, the bus goes to the railroad station. Maybe Graham is going away!"

Sue was so excited that she jumped up and down, shouting, "Let's go! Let's go!"

"All right," Mrs. Hollister agreed. "Call down to Dad that we're going downtown while I get the car out."

She hurried out and backed the station wagon from the garage. The girls ran out the back door of the house and hopped into the car. Pam held Sue on her lap so all could sit in the front seat. A minute later, Mrs. Hollister was on the main street, headed for the railroad station.

"Oh, dear!" Pam exclaimed as they had to stop for a red light. "If that bus gets too far ahead of us, Graham may leave on the train before we can see him."

Realizing this, Mrs. Hollister drove as fast as the law permitted, but met two more red lights before she reached the center of town.

"We'll get there in time, I believe," she said as they neared the station.

Just then they heard the siren of a fire engine. Immediately Mrs. Hollister pulled the car over to the curb.

"Goodness!" she said. "I hope we won't be delayed too long."

"Where are the engines?" Holly asked. "There's nothing ahead of us, Mother."

Pam glanced into the rear-view mirror. "Nor in back of us, either."

But the sound of the fire engines grew louder and soon a hook and ladder, then a pumper truck turned the corner directly in front of them. The hook and ladder truck pulled up close to Mrs. Hollister's car, blocking the way.

Two more engines roared up behind them, cutting off any possible retreat. The chief arrived in a bright red car, which his driver parked across the street. The girls gaped in wonder as the firemen hopped off the trucks and raced into the very building before which the Hollisters were parked!

"I want to see the fire!" cried Sue, forgetting their errand to tell Graham Stone about the hobbyhorse before the boy left town.

"But Graham may get away, and we can't walk to the station in time to catch the next train," her mother pointed out. "Let's speak to the chief and see if we can move our car."

Everyone left the car, and Mrs. Hollister took Sue and Holly by the hand. Glancing up, they could see smoke coming from the third floor of the three-story building. While the chief barked orders, more firemen hurried inside carrying hose and axes.

When the chief at last stood alone, Mrs. Hollister approached him. "Our station wagon is hemmed in by your apparatus," she said. "Is there any way we can get out?"

"Sorry, ma'am," the chief replied. "Not until the fire is out. We can't move our trucks right now. You were just unlucky to be parked in the wrong spot."

"Well, I hate to bother you," said Mrs. Hollister, "but it's important that we get to the station immediately."

"It's mostest important!" Sue said, looking up into the fireman's face.

"Then I'll have my deputy drive you there," he said. "Come with me."

"Thank you so much," said Mrs. Hollister gratefully. "We'll get our own car later."

The chief led them across the street to where his shiny red automobile stood, its motor running. At the wheel sat a good-looking young fireman.

"Jack," the chief said, "take these folks to the station immediately. We've got their car blocked."

The young man nodded, then reached back to open the rear door of the red car. Mrs. Hollister and her three daughters stepped in. As the car started up, its siren sounded, making chills run up and down the girls' spines.

"Wheeeee! This is fun!" Holly exclaimed.

"What excitement!" Pam added. "Pete and Ricky will be sorry they missed this!"

The chief's car was very fast and reached the station in two minutes. A train stood there.

"Oh, hurry!" Holly urged.

Mrs. Hollister thanked the driver as she opened the door. She and the girls quickly stepped out. Pam led the way through the station

"Graham! Graham! Wait!"

and looked up and down. The train suddenly began to move.

"There's Graham!" she cried excitedly, pointing to a boy who was just swinging himself onto the steps of one of the forward cars.

"Graham! Graham! Wait!" Holly screamed, dashing toward him.

The youth paused on the step a moment, then disappeared inside the car. As the train picked up speed, it left Mrs. Hollister and her daughters standing despairingly beside the tracks.

"Why do you suppose he wouldn't stop to talk with us?" Pam asked. She looked crestfallen.

"Maybe he couldn't wait for another train," Holly answered.

"It certainly is mysterious," their mother commented. "But maybe Graham didn't recognize us."

As they walked back inside the station, Pam said, "Perhaps the ticket agent can tell us where Graham is going and we can write to him."

Mrs. Hollister inquired at the counter, but the agent said that no young man had bought a ticket for that train. "Perhaps he had a return ticket to the place he came from," the man suggested.

"Where was the train going?" Holly asked.

"To the southern states."

"Then Graham *was* going home," Pam declared. "But where is that?"

The four Hollisters took a taxi back to the place where they had left the station wagon. The fire had been put out and the apparatus was just leaving the scene.

The chief approached them. "I thought you were taking a train," he said, puzzled.

Mrs. Hollister smiled. "We were trying to keep somebody else from taking one. You were kind to help us."

"Not at all," smiled the chief. "After all, *I* inconvenienced you in the first place." Mrs. Hollister and the girls returned to their car.

When they arrived home, Pam was the first to enter the house. What a hubbub was coming from the cellar!

"What's the matter?" Pam called down.

"We've just made a terrific discovery," Pete replied. "Come on down and look!"

Pam hurried down the steps, followed by her mother and sisters. Mr. Hollister and the boys stood before the workbench, on which lay the two halves of the rocking horse.

"They've operated on Mystery Boy," Holly giggled.

"Did he have 'pendicitis?" Sue asked. She turned toward the stairs, adding, "I'll get my nurse kit and help you put poor hobbyhorse back together."

"No need for that," Mr. Hollister said, reaching

down to pick Sue up. "Mystery Boy had a secret inside him. Look and see."

"Yikes, what we found!" Ricky exclaimed. "A lot of machinery."

Indeed there was! In what might be called the hobbyhorse's stomach was a series of wheels and gears. The girls gazed at them, wide-eyed.

"What are they for?" Pam said, curious.

"It's a rather elaborate balancing mechanism," her father replied. "You touch a certain button and the horse keeps rocking for some time. Quite an invention."

"What's the engineering principle that makes it work, Dad?" Pete asked.

Mr. Hollister studied the horse carefully and replied, "A gear train is connected to a pendulum with a heavy weight which is suspended at the end of it. The swinging of the pendulum makes a similar movement *in* the gear train. This causes the rockers to move."

"I don't understand one word of it," Pam laughed, "but what a clever idea!"

"And here's something else," Ricky said. "Dad found this inside the horse, too." He opened his hand in which he held a rolled-up piece of paper and spread it out on the workbench.

"What is that?" Holly asked.

"The plan of this valuable invention!" Mr. Hollister explained. "I've seen many hobbyhorses

65

in my day, but never one with anything so unusual as Mystery Boy. When we find Graham we'll tell him all about it. If he can find a buyer, this invention may make him rich."

"I'll bet this is the treasure everyone said was hidden in the old farmhouse!" cried Pete.

The girls groaned when they heard this.

"Graham's gone away," Pam said.

"We may never see him again," Holly sighed.

CHAPTER 7

JOEY'S REPORT

"WE HAVE to find Graham!" Pete Hollister said. "This invention may bring him a lot of money."

Mr. Hollister turned to his wife and daughters. "Are you sure it was Graham who left on the train?" he asked.

"It really did look like him, Dad," Pam said, and the others agreed.

"Then maybe we can still find him," her father said. "I have an idea!"

He suggested that they telephone the railroad station in the next big city. The stationmaster could have Graham paged by the conductor when the train stopped there.

"May I make the call, Dad?" Pete asked.

"Certainly."

Pete put in a long-distance call and told the stationmaster why he wanted to get a message to

67

Graham Stone. "Will you please have him contact us if he's on the train from Shoreham?" Pete asked the man.

The stationmaster said he would, and if Graham were not on the train, he would let the Hollisters know. Pete asked the railroad man when it would arrive and was told in an hour.

The hands of the clock seemed to crawl around the dial as the children waited impatiently for word about their new-found friend. An hour and a half later, the telephone rang. Pete ran to answer it. The call was from the stationmaster.

"We paged Graham Stone on the train, but nobody by that name spoke up," he told the boy.

"Then he wasn't on the train?"

"Seems not," the man replied, "unless he didn't want to identify himself."

When Pete reported this to his family, Pam said at once, "Graham seemed too honest a person to be like that."

All of them were disappointed and concluded it wasn't Graham who had left Shoreham.

"Then the person who got on the train looked enough like him to be his twin brother!" Mrs. Hollister declared.

Pete vowed that they would not give up their sleuthing. "If Graham's still in town, we'll find him tomorrow," the boy said.

Early next morning Pete and Ricky rode their

bicycles to police headquarters. They went straight to Officer Cal, a nice young policeman who had worked on several mysteries with the Hollister children.

Pete told their story, then asked, "Will you try to help us locate Graham Stone?"

"Sure I'll help!" said Officer Cal. The two boys gave a description of the youth, and Officer Cal said he would contact hotels, motels, and boarding houses around town.

"I'll also have the prowl cars keep on the lookout for him," he said, smiling. "If Graham Stone is in Shoreham, we'll find him."

The officer asked the brothers to get in touch with him in an hour for a report. Pete and Ricky said they would return to headquarters.

"Let's help Dad at the Trading Post while we're waiting," Pete suggested.

"Okay."

Two minutes later, they were in their father's store. It was a large place on the main street of town. The front show windows displayed all kinds of hardware, toys, and sporting goods.

Entering the front door, Pete called out, "Hi, Dad! I'm here to help pay back the money you lent me for the hobbyhorse."

"Me, too," said Ricky, who wanted to do his part. Buying the horse had been his idea.

Mr. Hollister smilingly said they were just in

time. "I was unpacking a carton of roller skates in the back of the store," he said. "Suppose you boys finish the job."

Before starting this, the boys went to speak to two men who worked at the Trading Post. They were Indy Roades, a real Indian from out west, and Tinker, an elderly man. Both were greatly liked by the Hollister children, and both had helped them solve some of their mysteries.

"Any new adventures?" Indy asked, his face crinkling into a smile.

Ricky told him about Graham, and the Indian said, "Let me know if I can help."

"We will, thanks."

Pete started for the back of the store. "Come on, Ricky, let's get these skates unpacked," he called.

His brother followed, and they started to remove the small boxes of skates from the large carton. Ricky could not resist opening one and pulling out a pair.

"Gee, Pete, these are keen!" he exclaimed. Ricky ran his hand over the wheels, making them spin furiously.

"Wonderful ball bearings!" Pete agreed. "Let's not play with them, though. Dad only wants them unpacked."

"I'm just going to try on one skate!" Ricky replied.

"Be careful of it," Pete warned.

His brother attached the skate to his shoe and

rolled on it a bit. "I wonder how it would feel with two," the boy mused. "This one is really super."

As Pete continued to unpack the carton, Ricky tried on the second skate. Then, with a push on the counter, he rolled across the wooden floor.

"Hey, come back here!" Pete cried. "Dad has to sell those skates. If you use 'em, they'll be second-hand in no time."

But Ricky had given himself such a good push that he was going fast. He was headed for the open rear door of the Trading Post.

"I can't stop, Pete!" he exclaimed, teetering.

As Ricky pitched toward the doorway, Dave Mead, Pete's best friend walked in. There was a collision, and both boys went down.

Dave picked himself and Ricky up and laughed. "Hey, what's going on here?" he asked. "Is this a roller derby?"

Ricky grinned and started to take off the skates. "These new ones are really fast."

Dave, a good-looking, dark-haired boy who lived near the Hollisters, went directly to Pete. "Say, I have some news for you," he said in a low voice. "Do you know someone named Graham Stone?"

"Do we!" exclaimed Pete. "We're trying to find him, Dave!"

"Well, I don't think he wants to see you," Dave said, "after what Joey Brill told him."

"What do you mean?"

Dave said he had met Joey a short time before.

The bully had bragged about how he had got even with the Hollisters for buying the hobbyhorse at the auction.

"Joey learned that you invited Graham to stay at your house," Dave said. "He met Graham here in town and told him that you Hollisters were only fooling—that you didn't really want him to come to your house."

"Why that's not true!" cried Ricky.

"I know it isn't," Dave said. "But Joey told Graham you had changed your mind about him when you learned how poor he was."

"So that's why Graham didn't show up," Pete exclaimed. He told Dave the whole story.

"It certainly was mean of Joey to make such a tale up," Dave said indignantly.

Pete remarked that Graham really might have been on the train, but felt so hurt that he had not answered when the conductor paged him for the Hollisters.

"Oh, I'd like to punch that bully for this!" cried Ricky, doubling his fists.

Pete hurried to the front of the store to tell his father what Joey Brill had done. Mr. Hollister frowned, then said, "Don't worry too much about it. Joey's very unreliable. Maybe he's giving Dave a phony story, too."

"That's right," Pete agreed. "He could have made up the whole thing."

Dave helped the boys unpack the carton of

skates. When they finished, all three went back to see Officer Cal.

"Your friend Graham has apparently left town," was the officer's report. "We've checked everywhere. But we'll keep on searching."

Pete thanked the officer, and the boys went back to the Trading Post. Mr. Hollister had several jobs for them to do, but before Pete went back to work he telephoned Pam and told her the discouraging report about Graham.

"Oh, dear," she sighed. "I wonder if we'll ever find him."

After Pam hung up, she told the story to Holly, who was standing beside her. Suddenly she brightened. "Maybe Joey Brill knows where Graham is!"

"I'd like to talk to Joey myself!" Holly said. "Let's go find him."

The girls told Mrs. Hollister where they were going, then ran almost all the way to the Brill home. Joey was in the backyard playing with his friend Will Wilson.

As the girls walked toward them, Joey scowled. "Get off our property!" he ordered.

"Not until I ask you a question," Pam said without moving. "Do you know where Graham Stone is?" She repeated the story she had heard from her brother.

"You did tell it to Dave Mead, didn't you?" asked Holly.

"Ha ha, that's all a big joke!" Joey said, giving

them a wise look. "I was just kidding Dave when I told him that."

"You mean you didn't speak to Graham?" Pam said.

"Sure I did, but I wouldn't tell a Hollister anything!"

"Please tell us!" Holly begged. "Because we have very important news for Graham."

Joey glanced slyly at Will Wilson. Then he said, "All right, I'll tell you where he is. Graham is living in a tent on Blackberry Island."

"Blackberry Island!" exclaimed Pam. "Why would he live there when he can stay with us?" Both boys shrugged in reply.

"Let's go to Blackberry Island and find Graham," Holly said to Pam, tossing her pigtails.

"You won't be able to—he's hiding in a secret place," Joey said. "But I'll tell you what. I'll take you girls there in your canoe."

Pam and Holly were afraid of some trick and said they would go there themselves.

"You'll never find him," Will spoke up.

"We can try," said Pam and walked out of the yard. Holly followed.

The boys ran after them. When they reached the Hollister dock, Joey plunked himself into the middle of the family canoe. "Come on," he urged.

Though both girls could swim, they would not think of going as far as Blackberry Island, which was in the middle of Pine Lake, without telling

"Stop that! We'll tip over."

their mother. But they did not want to leave Joey and Will there alone. The two boys might go off in the canoe!

Pam decided to try something—she would pretend to start with Holly for the island but stay in shallow water. Joey would become annoyed and go off.

"You get out," she said to him.

"I will not."

"All right," Pam said, pretending to be resigned to his accompanying them. "We'll start for Blackberry Island."

Joey turned to Will. "You stay here. I won't be gone long."

"How true!" thought Pam. She could hardly keep from giggling as she got into the bow of the canoe and said aloud, "I'll paddle you over!"

"No silly girl's going to paddle me!" Joey cried. "You and Holly sit in the stern."

Pam did not reply. She held onto the dock.

Suddenly Joey jumped out. He bent down, grabbed the end of the canoe and began tossing it up and down violently.

"Stop that!" Pam cried, trying to grab the dock again. "We'll tip over!"

"Let go, Will!" screamed Holly, as Joey's friend rushed over to help the bully.

As they tilted the canoe from side to side, the girls tried to keep their balance. But it overturned.

Splash! Pam and Holly pitched headlong into the lake water.

As Joey and Will turned to flee, a man hurried across the Hollisters' back lawn.

"Here, here, what's going on?" he cried out, running onto the wooden dock.

Joey tried to dodge out of his way, but the man reached out and collared the bully. As he did this, Will made his escape and a moment later was out of sight.

"I saw you throw those two girls into the water!" the man said sternly. "You can't do that to my cousins!"

Joey, looking frightened, wiggled violently. Pam and Holly stared at the man in amazement. They had never seen him before!

CHAPTER 8

AN EXCITING INVITATION

WITH a hard pull, Joey managed to slip from the grasp of the stranger who had said he was the Hollisters' cousin. As Joey raced off, the man turned to help Pam and Holly from the water and tie the canoe.

"I'm Charles Thomas," he said. "My wife is your mother's cousin, Ruth."

Pam and Holly smiled. "We're glad to meet you," they said, and Pam added, "Thank you for scaring those mean boys away."

"How did you know us, Mr. Thomas?" Holly asked, shaking the water off her pigtails.

"From pictures your mother has sent us. And by the way, call me Chuck," he said, grinning and walking toward the house with the sisters. "Everybody does."

Mr. Thomas was a thin man of medium height, with sandy hair, laughing blue eyes, and a ruddy, outdoor complexion. As they reached the rear porch of the house, Mrs. Hollister opened the door. She looked in amazement at her dripping wet daughters, then her face broke into a smile as she saw the man with them.

"Chuck Thomas!" she exclaimed. "What a nice surprise!"

"Hello, Elaine! I had unexpected business in town and thought I'd drop over to see you. Ruth was going to write you a special letter but I brought the message in person. And what a reception!" he laughed. "These two girls being dumped into the water!"

"Joey and Will did it," Pam said and told the whole story.

"I'm sure Graham isn't on the island," their mother commented. "Well, go get into dry clothes."

Pam and Holly ran into the house and up to their room. By the time they came downstairs, their mother was engaged in lively conversation with Chuck Thomas.

"Tell me all about your family," she said, as the girls sat down.

Chuck Thomas said that Ruth was fine and so were the two children.

"How old are they now?" Mrs. Hollister asked.

"Dan is twelve and Carol eight," Chuck replied. "You girls would like them."

The visitor explained that he had flown to Shoreham from a horse farm which he had purchased a short time before. It was several hundred miles away. "It's called Pony Hill Farm."

"What a cute name!" said Holly, who loved anything pertaining to horses.

"What kind of horses do you have?" Pam asked.

"We raise ponies and quarter horses," Chuck replied, "and we have a lot of fun doing it. There was a stock sale near Shoreham today. That's what brought me here."

"Did you buy anything?" Holly questioned.

"Two horses," their cousin replied. "They're being shipped to Pony Hill Farm."

"Please stay to dinner and be our guest overnight," Mrs. Hollister said. "John will want to see you."

"I want to see him, too," came a little voice from the hall. Everyone glanced toward the stairs. Little Sue was walking down, holding her shoes in one hand.

"This is the youngest Hollister," said her mother, introducing Sue. "She has just finished her nap. Come here, dear."

At first Sue approached a little shyly and sat on her mother's lap while Mrs. Hollister buckled her shoes. Then she edged slowly toward Chuck and in a few minutes was sitting on his knee.

"Do you have real live ponies on your farm?" the little girl asked.

"Yes, and I know you'd like to ride one of them," Chuck said, smiling.

Sue told about the hobbyhorse that Pam and Pete had bought her. "If I practice on Mystery Boy, I'll be able to ride real ponies like yours," said Sue. "You certainly will!" smiled Chuck.

When Pete and Ricky arrived home with Mr.

Hollister, they enjoyed meeting their cousin as much as their sisters had.

"He's so full of fun!" Pam whispered to Pete. "I wonder if his children are like him?"

Pam wondered why they had not heard more about Dan and Carol before and took her mother aside to ask about this. Mrs. Hollister explained that her cousin Ruth, and Chuck Thomas had been married only two years. Ruth had been a school teacher for several years before this. After they were married they adopted Dan and Carol, who were orphans attending Ruth's school.

"Isn't that wonderful!" Pam exclaimed. "Are Dan and Carol brother and sister?"

"Yes," said her mother.

At this moment Ricky was saying, "Think of living on a pony farm! Dan and Carol are lucky kids."

"Ruth and I are fortunate in having them," Chuck smiled.

The Hollisters' cousin continued to entertain the children with various stories about the farm until dinner time and all during the meal.

Finally Sue said, "It must be the bestest place in the whole world."

Chuck smiled, "Ruth and I would like to give you a chance to find out. How about coming to visit us soon?"

"Sure!" Ricky exclaimed enthusiastically.

Mr. and Mrs. Hollister exchanged glances, but

before they had a chance to reply, all five children were accepting the invitation at once.

Their cousin roared with laughter. "You'll have to make it unanimous," he said, grinning at Mr. and Mrs. Hollister.

"We'll do that," the children's father said. "When would you like us to come?"

Chuck said that the stock farms in the area where Pony Hill Farm was were having a special pony-day exhibition in about two weeks. "It would be fun for you to see that," he said. "All the events are for children. I know that the Hollisters would have a great time."

Just then a voice from the nearest window startled everybody. "If you want some fun, you should go!" it said.

"Why, who's that?" Mrs. Hollister asked, looking up.

Pete jumped up from the table and ran to the window. "I can't see anybody," he said, mystified.

Quickly excusing themselves, the children raced out of the house and searched the shrubbery beneath the window from which the voice had come. They returned a few minutes later.

"We couldn't find anybody," Holly said. "He must have run away."

"Who could it have been?" Pam asked, perplexed.

"Probably one of your playmates," Mrs. Hollister suggested.

Chuck Thomas smiled, "It might have been a

gremlin or an elf. But what he said was right. If you want to have some fun, you should come to Pony Hill Farm."

"We'll be there all right," Pete assured him.

Chuck told them about the fields and paddocks and stables where the animals were kept. "You'll enjoy knowing Ben and Melinda, the elderly couple who work for me," he added. "You'll love them. They help us plant and cultivate our gardens, and Ben grooms the animals."

Shortly before bedtime, the Hollisters and their guest sat on the screened-in porch, enjoying the long summer evening. Chuck told them that he would have to leave early in the morning, and Mr. Hollister said he would drive him to the airport.

Mr. Thomas turned to the boys, a twinkle in his eyes. "What are you going to do about that fellow who dumped your sisters into the lake?" he asked.

"I'd like to play a trick on him!" Pete said.

Suddenly Ricky let out a yippee. "I know what we can do!" he said.

"What?" all the children asked at once.

Ricky chuckled to himself and said, "I'll whisper it to Chuck, and if he likes it, I'll tell you all tomorrow."

"Oh, please tell us now," Holly begged.

"No, it's going to be a surprise," Ricky said importantly and took their cousin aside. Chuck laughed heartily. "That's a good one," he said.

At Mrs. Hollister's request all the children said

83

good night and went off to bed. By the time they came down to breakfast the next morning, their father already had driven Chuck to the airport.

"He's such a nice man!" Pam said. "I just can't wait to visit Pony Hill Farm."

"But before we do, we're going to get even with Joey Brill!" Ricky said. While his brother and sisters listened, he told of his plan.

"Oh good! I know just the thing!" Pam said when Ricky finished. "Mother has some old sheets in a rag bag in the attic."

While the Hollister children were getting ready for their joke, Joey Brill felt very content about the mean stunt he had played on Pam and Holly. He was sitting in the living room of his home, watching a morning television program with Will Wilson.

"Ha ha," Joe was saying. "It will take Pam and Holly a long time to find Graham Stone. I got 'em all wet so they didn't even go to Blackberry Island to look."

"They'll never find out," Will chuckled.

Suddenly there was a loud rapping on the front door.

"Answer it, Will," Joey ordered.

"It's your door," Will snapped. "You answer it."

"Oh, all right," Joey said.

He opened the door and looked around. No one was in sight. But at his feet lay a white envelope with his name on it. Joey picked it up and came back inside.

"Look, Will. A letter for me," he said.

"What's it say?"

"Turn that TV down and I'll read it to you," Joey said, tearing open the envelope.

The letter inside made him whistle. "Listen to this, Will.

"*The treasure in the old Stone farm house is waiting for you. If you don't go for it immediately, I'll tell the Hollisters where it is.*

"*Mr. X*"

On the reverse side of the paper was a drawing of the old house. A dotted line led through the front door, up the steps and to a closet in a back bedroom.

"Someone's trying to play a trick on you," Will said.

"I don't know about that," Joey replied. "If we don't go for the treasure, the Hollisters might get there ahead of us. Come on, Will. We'll go out together."

"Not me," his friend said.

"What's the matter? Scared?"

"Not exactly," Will said uneasily. "But I've heard too many crazy stories about that old place. You can go out there alone."

"Who, me?" Joey said, a bit hesitant.

"Sure, you're a brave guy," Will taunted him. "You're not afraid of anything, are you?"

"Well, no, I guess not," Joey said, screwing up his courage.

"Then go alone. I'll watch television until you get back."

"Oh, I'll go some time later," Joey said nervously.

"Go on now!" Will teased. "Don't tell me you're afraid of ghosts!"

"Course I'm not," Joey replied. He stomped out of the house and down the front steps. Then, jumping on his bike, he sped off.

Fifteen minutes later he pulled up in front of the old farmhouse and propped his bike against a tree. Nobody was in sight. Joey approached the house cautiously.

As he mounted the front steps, they squeaked and creaked. Joey stopped and listened. He was almost too afraid to go on, but the thought of the Hollisters getting the treasure prodded him. The boy tiptoed through the front door, which stood wide open, and climbed the stairs as quietly as possible.

Suddenly a tinkling bell startled him. "What's that?" he called out.

The only reply was an echo in the empty rooms. The bully started to shake. He would have run back down the stairs but he was too close to the treasure.

As Joey entered the room he thought he heard a

They lifted their arms and moaned "Whoooooo!"

low moan. His teeth chattered. "M-m-maybe there *is* a real ghost here after all," he said to himself as he advanced toward the closet door.

Just then a deep, faraway voice said, "Before you can have the treasure, you must tell where Graham Stone is."

Joey jumped. "I—I don't know. He went away on a train."

"If you are telling the truth, you may open the door," the deep voice told him.

Joey put his hand gingerly on the doorknob. It clicked as he turned it. With his heart pounding, Joey flung the door open then gave a yell of fright.

Two white-clad figures stood before him! They lifted their arms and moaned "Whooooooooo!"

"Ghosts!" Joey screamed.

He turned and fled down the stairs, the two figures after him. Halfway to the bottom he tripped and tumbled.

Bangity bump! Joey landed on the first floor, picked himself up, and dashed across the porch. After racing over the lawn, he jumped on his bicycle and sped off.

CHAPTER 9

A DANGEROUS DRIVER

JOEY BRILL bent over his handlebars and pedaled the bike as fast as he could. He did not dare to glance back at the house, where two white-garbed figures stood on the porch.

When Joey was out of sight, they pulled white sheets from over their heads.

The ghosts were Pete and Ricky Hollister!

Ricky was laughing so hard that tears of mirth ran down his cheeks.

"How do you like that?" Pete said, chuckling. "Our brave friend is really afraid of ghosts."

"He didn't even wait to get the treasure," Ricky chuckled, holding up a cheap play watch.

"And we found out Graham Stone isn't on Blackberry Island and he did take a train," Pete said. "This was a good morning's work."

"I guess it *was* Graham Mother and the girls saw," Ricky added. "It'll be pretty hard to find him now." Then he said, "Now that we got square with Joey, we can go to Pony Hill Farm."

"Joey got what was coming to him," Pete agreed.

Folding up the sheets and tucking them under their arms, the boys walked around to the back of the house, where their bicycles were hidden in the bushes. As soon as they arrived home, the brothers told the others what had happened.

Everyone laughed except Sue, who said, "I hope Joey didn't get hurted like me when he fell down the steps."

"The way he raced off I'm sure he wasn't hurt," Pete chuckled.

Presently the children left the house to play near the waterfront. A few minutes later, Donna Martin ran up to Holly. The dimpled, brown-eyed girl, who lived a few doors away, was Holly's age and her special friend.

"Guess what?" Donna said, out of breath. "Joey Brill was chased by ghosts."

Holly glanced at her brothers and giggled. Pete returned a wink and shook his head, advising her to keep what she knew a secret.

"Really?" Holly replied. "Where?"

"At old Mr. Stone's house," Donna replied. "Joey says he's never going out there again and everybody should stay away."

Later that day the Hollisters heard the same story from several other friends. But they did not let on that it was the Hollister boys who had frightened the bully. Sometime they would tell them, and Joey too, but right now they wanted to avoid any tricks he might play to get square.

Preparations for their trip to Pony Hill Farm kept the family busy for the next few days. Mr. Hollister arranged to leave his business in charge of Indy Roades and Tinker. Jeff and Ann Hunter agreed to take care of Domingo, White Nose, and the kittens. Zip would go along on the trip.

Finally the morning came for the Hollisters to depart. The back of their station wagon was crammed with suitcases. Sue and her mother climbed into the front seat with Mr. Hollister. His wife would spell with the driving. The other children took seats in the back, as did Zip.

"Hurray, here we go!" Ricky called out, as his father backed out of the driveway.

"It shouldn't take very many hours to get to Pony Hill Farm," Mr. Hollister said after they were rolling on the open road.

"How far is it?" Pete asked.

"About two hundred and fifty miles."

There was so much to see along the lovely countryside on this warm, late June day that the morning passed quickly. After eating a picnic lunch by the roadside, the Hollisters continued on their way.

Pete kept looking at a road map spread on his lap. Mr. Hollister, who was at the wheel now, called back, "How are we doing, navigator?"

His son replied that they should turn right at the next intersection. "There's a black-top road we must take for several miles. Then left onto a dirt road which leads to Pony Hill Farm."

"Roger, skipper," and Mr. Hollister proceeded as his son directed.

Some time later Pete called, "Here's the dirt road, Dad. Turn left here."

"It certainly is narrow," Mrs. Hollister remarked as they pulled into it. "And dusty, too."

"Yikes, we'll soon be there!" Ricky exclaimed.

"Look," Holly suddenly remarked, pointing.

Far up ahead a cloud of dust indicated that an automobile was traveling at high speed. In a moment they could see the car tearing toward them. "It's hauling a small horse van!" Mrs. Hollister observed.

"The poor horses!" said Pam, for the car was going so fast that the van behind swayed from side to side.

"I'm going to pull off to the side of the road," her father said. "I don't trust that driver. He's acting like a maniac!"

Quickly Mr. Hollister pulled over to the right in the shade of a big oak tree. He ordered the windows rolled shut so dust wouldn't blow in their car. "Now Mr. Speedy can have the whole road," he told the others.

As the car sped past, the Hollisters could see that fortunately the van was empty. But it still

The empty horse van swayed dangerously.

swayed dangerously and sent up a shower of dust and gravel onto the station wagon.

"Crickets!" Pete exclaimed. "You couldn't see who was driving."

The man was bending so low over the steering wheel he could not be recognized. A fellow sitting next to him covered his face with a hand as they passed.

"Maybe they're escaping from somebody," Ricky suggested. "Do you suppose the police were chasing them?"

"I don't know," his father replied, "but we'll soon find out." No police car showed up, however, and finally Mr. Hollister steered the station wagon back onto the road.

Five minutes later, Pete announced, "Only three miles to go!" This made the other children so excited that they sang over and over, "Hi-ho! Hi-ho! To Pony Hill Farm we go!"

"I see it!" Ricky exclaimed.

Ahead and to the right of the road was a big sign painted in bright colors. *Entrance to Pony Hill Farm*. An arrow on it pointed down a lane.

Mr. Hollister made the turn and drove up a slight incline. Finally they could see the white fences which enclosed the paddocks of the pony farm.

"What a beautiful place!" Mrs. Hollister remarked. Off to the left of the lane was a lovely white farmhouse with green shutters, and across

94

the road from it were several low barns with meadows beyond.

"Look at all the horses!" Sue cried out, pointing to several sleek animals in a nearby field.

"Here come our cousins," Pam said seeing the farmhouse door open and four people run out. Chuck, in the lead, hurried toward the Hollisters. Behind him was a smiling woman with dark, curly, close-cut hair. Running beside her were two rosy-cheeked children.

Mr. Hollister stopped the car and everyone piled out. Zip ran around barking joyfully. Introductions were quickly made, and Mrs. Hollister embraced her cousin Ruth.

"Elaine, I'm so glad you and your family could come," said Ruth, her dark eyes sparkling.

"And Dan and I are too," said Carol, who was a little taller than Holly but shorter than Pam. She was dressed in jeans and low-cut riding boots.

Dan, who was Pete's age, was dressed the same. He was not so broad-shouldered as the Hollister boy, but slightly taller. The boy had a shock of brown hair and generous freckles. Both he and his sister were very suntanned from outdoor living.

"We'll take you to our guesthouse," Ruth said.

"What a nice surprise!" Mrs. Hollister replied, laughing. "You didn't tell me you had a guesthouse."

"We've just built it," her cousin said. "And you're our first guests to use it. Come, I'll show you where it is."

Behind the farmhouse and off to one side stood a gleaming white cottage. It had four bedrooms, two baths, and a small sitting room. The Hollisters' baggage was brought in.

After they had washed the dust from their hands and faces, the Hollisters told Chuck and his family about the speeding car and horse van.

"That driver ought to be reported," Mr. Hollister declared.

Chuck said he did not believe the van belonged to anyone living near them, and added, "I hope that driver never comes back." Then he said, "Now we'll show you the farm. First I'll introduce you to Ruth's babies."

"Babies!" Sue shouted. "Oh, I love babies."

Ruth laughed and explained to the little girl that these weren't human babies.

"I call our horses my babies," she said with a chuckle.

"Let's show them Pat and Mike first," Carol said, skipping on ahead. She led them into a barn which was lined with box stalls on both sides. Opening one of them, Carol pointed to two black Shetland ponies, about the size of the Hollisters' hobbyhorse.

"They're twins," she said, and Dan added, "We're training them to pull a carriage in one of the Pony Day events."

The Hollister children petted the Shetland ponies, declaring they were cute and pretty.

"They ought to take a prize," Mrs. Hollister remarked.

"Now look at what we have over here," Chuck remarked, leading the way to the other side of the barn as Dan closed the door of the stall.

In a larger stall stood a beautiful chestnut horse. "This is Duke," Chuck explained. "He's a quarter horse."

At this remark Sue giggled. "Oh, Chuck, you're teasing us," she said. "It really isn't."

"Isn't what?" her cousin asked.

"A quarter of a horse," the small girl explained. "Duke's a whole horse."

Everyone laughed, and Dan said, "A quarter horse is a certain breed of western pony. They have big chests and strong legs. Their powerful hind-quarters give them added running strength and speed."

The boy pointed out that this special breed could start a race very fast and outrun almost any other kind of horse for a quarter of a mile.

"So that's why they're called a quarter horse," Holly said.

Chuck explained that a thoroughbred horse could beat a quarter horse in a long race, but for work in the cow country a quarter horse is the best kind.

"Duke," said Carol, "is also a trick horse. We'll show you some time."

As they made a tour of the barns and paddocks,

Dan told his cousins about the thrilling horseback races they had had against children from neighboring farms.

"There's going to be a keen quarter-horse race on Pony Day," the boy remarked.

"Will Duke ride in it?" Pete asked.

"Sure thing!" grinned Dan. "And I'm going to be the jockey."

"Please give me a ride on Duke," Holly begged.

"Do you ride well?"

Pete answered for his sister by saying that they had all ridden horses on a ranch out west.

Dan explained he had asked this question because sometimes Duke was difficult to ride. "But if you've ridden western horses, you won't have any trouble," he told Holly.

While their parents were inspecting another part of the farm, the children returned to the stall, where Carol and Dan saddled Duke. Then Dan led the horse into a paddock behind the barn.

"Be careful, Holly," Carol said, as Holly put her foot into the stirrup and swung herself up. "This horse is very fast. Start him slowly."

But Holly, happy to be on the quarter horse, had already nudged Duke with her heels and said, "Giddap!"

Zoom! The beautiful animal sprang forward so fast that Holly was thrown backward and jolted from the saddle!

CHAPTER 10

LARIAT TOSSERS

As PETE ran toward the horse, Holly gave a startled cry and tumbled off his back. She landed sitting down on the soft turf. While Pete and Pam helped their sister up, Dan gave a shrill whistle.

Duke skidded to an abrupt halt, then turned around and trotted back to his master.

"You shouldn't have started off so fast," Dan scolded the horse. "Holly's not used to four-legged thunderbolts!"

Duke hung his head and pawed the ground as Carol added, "Aren't you ashamed of yourself?"

The quarter horse bobbed his head up and down, looking so funny that Holly forgot her bump and began to laugh.

"It was really my fault," she confessed, "for not paying attention to what Carol started to say. Besides, I wasn't holding the reins tight enough." Holly patted Duke as she said this.

"Get right back on Duke," Carol suggested, not wanting Holly to fear riding the trick horse.

In a moment Holly was in the saddle once more. Duke started out slowly. Then he broke into a trot and finally a gallop, with the girl riding well. When Holly returned to the group and dismounted, she sang his praises.

"I'd like to be a cowgirl if I could have a quarter horse like Duke!" she exclaimed happily.

It was nearly suppertime for the horses as well as the Thomases and their guests. The children helped feed the ponies and horses the hay and oats and brought water to the stalls.

When they finished, Carol showed the Hollisters the tack room where the saddles and bridles hung neatly from wooden pegs along the wall.

"There are so many of them!" Pam gasped.

In one corner of the room was a wardrobe in which hung fancy silk costumes of many colors. Carol explained that these were worn in costume events at the various horse shows which their father entered.

"We're going to have a costume event at Pony Day," she told the Hollisters.

"I just can't wait to see," Holly said.

Sue, who had not had a nap, yawned during supper and went to bed immediately afterward. But she was the first one up next morning in the guest cottage. After dressing quickly, Sue roused the others.

"Get up, sleepyheads," she giggled, prodding her sisters and brothers and rapping on her parents' bedroom door.

Then, while waiting for the others to dress and

go over to the main house for breakfast, Sue skipped to the paddock fence nearest the barn and climbed up on it. Cupping her chin in her hands, the little girl rested her elbows on the top rail and gazed fondly at the ponies inside the paddock.

Suddenly Sue gave such a start that she nearly fell off the fence. "Oh, oh!" she exclaimed. "It can't be real. But it is!"

Scrambling off the fence, Sue raced across the lane and into the guesthouse. "Mother! Daddy!" she cried out. "You have to come and see it!"

"See what, dear?" Mrs. Hollister asked as Sue burst into her room.

"Mystery Boy has come to life!" came the breathless reply.

"What's this?" her father asked as he slipped on a sports jacket.

"A horse. A real live hobbyhorse!" Sue explained.

"I don't think my little cricket is quite awake yet," Mr. Hollister said with a chuckle.

"But I am too!" the excited child replied, grasping her father's hand and pulling him toward the bedroom. "Come and I'll show you, Daddy."

The other Hollisters were also curious, and Sue led the family toward the paddock.

"Goodness, Sue's right!" Mrs. Hollister gasped.

In the center of the paddock stood a beautiful appaloosa pony. She was pure white with black dots, some large, some small.

"What a lovely animal!" Pam exclaimed.

"I didn't know our cousins had an appaloosa," Pete said. "I didn't see it yesterday."

Dan Thomas came running over. He said good morning, then stared into the paddock.

"A rare appaloosa!" he exclaimed. "Why that pony isn't ours!"

"Not yours?" the Hollisters chorused.

"Never saw her before," Dan added.

"Then how did she get in here?" Ricky asked.

"She probably jumped the fence," Dan replied. "But where did she come from?"

By this time his mother and father had joined the group, and all stood in amazement, admiring the appaloosa filly. Chuck said the animal was very valuable and he did not know of any neighbors who had one.

He climbed the fence and tried to get near the strange animal but she trotted away nervously.

"Get me a handful of hay," the farm owner requested, and Ricky ran for some.

But even this did not bring the appaloosa to Chuck. Finally he said, "I guess we'll have to rope her and look for a brand mark."

"Suppose she doesn't have one," Dan said. "Then what'll we do, Dad?"

Chuck smiled. "Let's not worry about that, son, until it's necessary. Right now I believe we should capture her so she won't run away."

They noticed that every once in a while the pony

would raise her left hind leg and try to reach the flank with her mouth.

"Something's bothering the pony," said Pam.

"We'll find out what it is as soon as we catch her," Carol replied.

Chuck put a hand on Pete's shoulder. "How about you and Dan playing cowboy and roping our visitor?"

"Yippee!" Pete cried, and Dan nodded. The boys hurried to the stable and a few minutes later returned astride two quarter horses. Chuck opened the gate to the paddock, and they rode in, lariats poised in their right hands.

"Take it easy," Dan called quietly, but as they approached the pony she kicked up her heels and galloped toward the far fence.

Spurring their horses in pursuit, Pete said, "I hope she doesn't jump over."

"Looks as if she might."

The appaloosa came to a sudden halt a few feet from the fence and turned around. At the same instant Pete's horse turned, so that the boy had a perfect lasso shot at the pony's head.

Floating through the air, the loop landed plump on the target. As Pete pulled the rope taut the appaloosa started off at a fast clip.

"Hang on tight!" Dan called out.

Pete tried but had not reckoned with the speed of the filly. Before the boy had a chance to snub

Pete clung desperately to the lariat.

the rope on the pommel of his saddle, he was jerked off his horse. Rolling over as he hit the ground, Pete was more startled than bruised.

He clung desperately to the lariat with the appaloosa pulling him swiftly along the ground.

A second later, Dan's lasso dropped over the animal's head and brought the pony to a sudden stop. "Are you O.K., Pete?" Dan called out.

"Sure," his cousin answered, picking himself up and brushing the dirt from his Levis. "Now I know how it feels to be a jet flier."

Dan dismounted and approached the captured pony with a friendly smile, talking to her in low tones. "There, there, old girl," he said. "Don't be afraid. You're in good hands."

The appaloosa pulled back her head as Dan tried to pet her. He did not rush the job, and in a few moments the runaway had lost her fear of him. She allowed herself to be led back to the paddock gate and seemed friendly when the others stroked her neck.

"That was a real cowboy act," Chuck praised the two young riders. "A splendid job!"

"It certainly was," Dan's mother complimented them as she went into the paddock and walked around the pony. "This filly is a prize animal," she remarked, noting the fine legs and chest.

As the appaloosa again tried to reach the left flank with her mouth, Carol exclaimed, "I see the reason! The pony has a splinter in her!"

"We'll have to attend to that immediately," Chuck said, "before the wound becomes infected."

"Do you see any marks of ownership on the pony?" Pam asked.

Dan and Carol examined the appaloosa carefully. But they could find no brand or other mark indicating to whom she belonged.

"It's certainly a mystery," said Chuck as he led the filly forward into a large stall in the stable. Then he went for a first-aid kit saying, "I wish I knew more about veterinary medicine."

"A boy we know named Graham Stone wants to be a veterinarian," Holly told the Thomases. While Ruth made the appaloosa lie down, she explained how they had met Mr. Stone's grandson. "But now we can't find him."

Chuck returned and the Hollister children watched, fascinated, as he drew the splinter from the pony's flank. Then his wife quickly applied an antiseptic to the wound.

"I wonder what the pony's name is," Ricky said as the appaloosa rose to her feet.

"Let's give her one," said Holly. She looked at the pony a moment then added, "There's a little black star on her forehead and——"

"I know!" interrupted Sue. "*Stardust* would be a good name 'cause she has a star and she kicked up so much dust when Pete and Dan tried to catch her."

"Stardust it is!" Ruth cried, hugging the little girl. "It's a pretty name."

Holly walked over to the pony. "Hello, Stardust," she said softly, touching the black star on the animal's forehead. The pony neighed.

"I think we should let the poor animal rest for a while," Chuck advised as he gathered up his kit. Then suddenly he squinted his eyes as he looked at the others. "Say, I wonder if this is an appaloosa talking pony?"

"A what?" Ricky asked, wrinkling his nose.

Chuck repeated his question and looked straight at the animal. "I didn't know there were any talking ponies," Ricky said.

Without explaining, Chuck said to Stardust, "What is your new name?"

"Stardust, sir," came the reply.

The Hollister children looked at the pony goggle-eyed.

"You see, she does talk!" their cousin said.

CHAPTER 11

HORSEBACK DETECTIVES

Looks of disbelief had come over the faces of the Hollister children when they heard Stardust reply to Chuck's question.

"She talks!" Holly exclaimed glancing at her brothers and sisters to be sure she had heard right. They nodded.

"How old are you? Do you like ice cream? What's your real name?" asked Sue along with other questions. The pony just looked at her.

A little smile crossed Pam's face, and she whispered something to Pete. Then Pam asked the horse, "Where did you come from, Stardust?"

The beautiful pony remained silent and shook her head back and forth. "Hmmmmmm, I guess the cat got her tongue," Chuck remarked. "By George, I didn't expect to find a talking appaloosa pony on my farm!"

Dan and Carol, meanwhile, had made no further comment about the filly's unusual talent. When the pony had replied to their father's question, they had looked the other way. The brother and sister acted as if talking ponies were a common thing in their lives!

"We have a lot to learn," thought Holly.

During the day all the children went to see Stardust every hour or so. Meanwhile, they did some detective work trying to locate the pony's owner. Dan and Carol telephoned all the farmers who lived nearby. None of them owned the appaloosa.

"I guess she came from farther away," Dan concluded. "But where?"

He and Carol took their cousins to meet Ben and Melinda. The elderly man was grooming a quarter horse, and after Pete had talked to him for ten minutes he concluded there was little the interesting man did not know about horses. And a while later he decided there was nothing which his round-faced, happy wife, Melinda, did not know about flowers and vegetables.

Later, as Pete was watching Chuck bed down the appaloosa pony for the night, he had an idea and said, "What did you do with the splinter you removed from Stardust?"

"I think Ruth dropped it in the straw."

"I'd like to see it," Pete said, and searched until he found the splinter.

"Why do you want it?" Chuck asked curiously.

"It might be a good clue," Pete replied. "Perhaps it will help lead us to Stardust's owner."

Dan, who had come into the stable, grinned. "Say, Pete how do you go about being a detective?"

"I'll show you," Pete answered. "Come with me." He led Dan to the little cottage where Ben and Melinda lived. The old man was hoeing tomato plants in his little dooryard garden.

"Hello, boys," he called out cheerfully. "Something I can do for you?"

Pete nodded. "You know a lot about horse vans, don't you?" he asked.

"Played around 'em since I was a boy," said Ben, stopping his work and leaning on the hoe.

Taking the splinter from his pocket, Pete said, "Would you say this came from a horse van?"

Ben took hold of the splinter and turned it over in his hands. "Why yes, I would say so," he answered. "Looks like piece of a tail gate from one of those old-type vans."

"Then I have a hunch that Stardust may have escaped from a van which nearly hit us when we were driving here!" cried Pete, his eyes lighting up with excitement.

Ben turned the splinter over in his hand.

"A good deduction!" Dan said admiringly. "I'll bet you're right. What do we do next?"

His cousin said that the next morning they would take the splinter and question neighboring farmers also. Hearing this, all the children wanted to help.

"Then let's break up into teams of two each," suggested Pete.

After breakfast the following day the four older Hollister children, Carol and Dan gathered in front of the stable.

"Playing detective is thrilling!" Carol said as Pete chose the teams.

Ricky and Dan would be one team, Pam and Holly the second pair, and Pete and Carol the third. Ruth had given them a list of various farms in the area. The children would ride to them and ask if anyone had seen the empty horse van.

"What if they did?" Carol wanted to know.

Pam explained that they should get a description of the car, the direction it was going and what the driver and the other man looked like.

"I'm sure we can turn up something," Dan said as they walked into the stable to saddle up.

Since he and Carol were familiar with the countryside, the only riders who needed directions were Holly and Pam. They would stop at two farms directly down the road. Carol told them one was half a mile, the other one mile.

All three groups of riders set off briskly from Pony Hill Farm, with Ricky riding Duke, his favorite. He and Dan took a short cut across the fields to Green Acre Farm. After going through a woods and splashing across a shallow stream, the boys came to the boundary of the farm.

"We'll rein in at the stables," said Dan. This they did, and a moment later a man came outside. They asked him whether he had seen the speedy car pulling the empty horse van.

"No, I haven't, but I'll be on the lookout for it," the farmer promised. "If I do spot the van I'll get in touch with you."

"Where do we go next?" Ricky asked Dan as they wheeled their horses about and started off.

"Mr. Jessup's farm, a couple of miles from here," Dan replied. "He raises thoroughbred horses."

When the boys arrived there they saw a kindly-looking, gray-haired man in a paddock exercising a jet-black mare.

"Howdy, Dan!" he called when he saw the callers. "Out for a ride today?"

"We're doing some detective work," Dan replied, and introduced Ricky to Mr. Jessup. Without dismounting, the boys told the horse breeder about their mission.

"An empty horse van?" Mr. Jessup said stroking his chin thoughtfully. "I do recall seeing one—oh, yes, now I remember."

He said that several days before he had been driving along the swamp road when a single horse van had nearly crowded him into a ditch.

"The same as the driver almost did to us!" Ricky exclaimed.

"Sure seemed to be a reckless driver," Mr. Jessup went on.

"Were there two men in the car?" Ricky asked.

"Yes, there were, but I didn't get a good look at them."

"Did you notice anything special that would give us a clue?" Dan went on.

"The van wasn't from this state," he said. "I could tell from the license plate."

"Where was it from?" Ricky asked.

"That I can't honestly say," Mr. Jessup replied, "because the car was going too fast and kicking up a fearful dust."

"That's still a good clue!" Ricky exclaimed. "Thanks a lot."

On the way back toward Pony Hill Farm, Dan said that the information might help the police track down the reckless driver.

Ricky nodded. "If Stardust was in that van at one time," he said, "those men might have been stealing her."

"Rustlers!" Dan cried excitedly. "Do you suppose we're on the trail of horse thieves?"

"Yikes!" Ricky exclaimed, feeling very important.

"But say, how do you suppose Stardust got out of the van?"

Dan said that perhaps the tail gate had fallen down and the pony had slid out onto the road. The two boys had skirted the edge of a cornfield and now were on a dirt lane leading back to Pony Hill Farm.

"Here comes a boy!" Ricky said, looking up the road.

"It's Sam Dulow," Dan remarked. He said that Sam was a strange, unpleasant fellow whose parents worked on a nearby farm.

Ricky noticed that Sam was a tall boy with black, disheveled hair. Dan added, "He frowns most of the time and seems mad at everything. Once in a while Sam punches the smaller kids for no reason at all."

"Like Joey Brill back home," Ricky remarked.

Dan and Ricky advanced on the opposite side of the road from Sam Dulow. But as they approached the boy, he ran up in front of their horses.

"Stop! I want to talk to you!" Sam cried out. He squinted his eyes, making a crease in his forehead.

"Hi, Sam!" Dan said.

"Who's the kid you've got with you?"

"Ricky Hollister. His family's staying with us for a while. Ricky, this is Sam Dulow."

"Hello, Sam."

The other boy ignored the introduction. "Did they bring the appaloosa pony with them?" he asked.

"No, we found her in our paddock," Dan said. "How did you know about Stardust?" he added.

"Oh, news travels around here," Sam said with a smirk. "I'd like to ride that appaloosa sometime."

"No one can ride her for a while," Dan said. "She was injured."

Sam reached up and pulled at Duke's reins. "Let me have a ride on him," he said.

Ricky glanced at Dan, not knowing whether to dismount or not.

As Dan hesitated, Sam said, "Come on—I won't hurt your old horse."

"Go ahead," Dan said reluctantly. "Let him have a ride, Ricky." Then he added, "Please don't gallop Duke, and bring him back in a few minutes."

Ricky hopped to the ground and Sam flung himself on the quarter horse. He started off at a trot. When he was fifty yards down the road he broke into a gallop.

"I told him not to do that!" Dan said angrily. "There are too many stones on the road."

About quarter of a mile farther on the boy turned around and began to gallop back. As he went past the boys Dan called out, "Sam, you've ridden enough. Give Ricky the horse!"

"Says who?" the boy replied rudely without pausing. "I want a longer ride."

"We have to get back to the farm," Dan said. "Let Ricky get on now."

Sam did not bother to reply, but wheeled Duke for another dash down the road.

"You'd better quit!" Dan said hotly.

"Try and stop me!" came the reply.

"All right, I will!" Dan cupped his hands and cried out to Duke, "Ride 'em, bronc!"

Instantly Duke stopped short, nearly throwing Sam over his head. Then he began a series of bucks and sunfishes as Sam held on for dear life. This was one of Duke's tricks.

"Stop him! Stop him! I'll get off!" Sam yelled.

"Have you had enough?" Dan called.

"Y-y-yes. Stop this critter!"

With a few quieting words, Dan calmed the beautiful quarter horse. Sam hopped off, trembling.

Ricky scrambled onto Duke's back, but before the boys could start off Sam shook his fist at them. "I'm going to get you for this!" he threatened. "I have friends who will make trouble for you!"

CHAPTER 12

SECRETS

AFTER Sam Dulow had made his threat, he ran down the road. Ricky and Dan spurred their mounts and continued toward Pony Hill Farm.

"Can Sam's friends do us any harm?" Ricky asked, a little fearful.

"I doubt it," Dan replied. "I think Sam was just bluffing. He doesn't seem to have many friends."

"Maybe that's why he acts so mad all the time," said Ricky.

Dan nodded. "My mother thinks the poor guy's lonely but is too proud to show it," Dan told him. "Another thing," he explained, "is that Sam is crazy about horses—the same as we all are around here. He's always talking about getting one but never does. Did you notice how well he rode Duke?"

"I sure did," said Ricky. "But that doesn't excuse him for running off with my horse. Why can't he buy his own?" Dan explained that Sam's parents could not afford to do this.

By the time Ricky and Dan arrived at Pony

Hill Farm the other four children were there. They had not turned up a single clue about the horse van and were very much interested to learn that Ricky and Dan had discovered it had an out-of-state license.

Mr. Thomas immediately went to telephone state-trooper headquarters and ask them to be on the lookout for an out-of-state horse van. He also told the captain about the clue of the splinter found in Stardust's side. After the officer promised to be on the lookout, Chuck hung up and returned to the stable. He reported the conversation, then changed the subject.

"Pony Day is only a week off," he told his young guests. "I think you Hollisters should enter the events."

"Oh goody!" cried Sue.

"I'd love to ride Stardust," Pam said enthusiastically. "Cousin Ruth thinks she'll be ready to saddle tomorrow. Then I can practice."

For the next few days the Hollisters did little but practice for Pony Day. Thoughts of the empty van and Sam Dulow's threat almost vanished from their minds.

Pete and Dan spent many hours trying trick riding. Dan showed his cousin how to stand up in the saddle while going at a gallop. And Chuck taught Pete the correct way to lean far over to one side and scoop up a handkerchief from the ground.

Carol and Ricky, meanwhile, practiced a rope-spinning act. The two children stood side by side, twirling tiny loops which they gradually increased in size until they were large enough for them to jump in and out of.

"You're wonderful!" Pam praised them.

Sue and Holly had decided to enter the costume event. Melinda came to the house regularly to help Mrs. Hollister make Gay Nineties costumes for them. Finally they were ready for a fitting. As Holly and Sue stood before a mirror, Melinda's brown eyes flashed happily as she adjusted one of the ruffles on the quaint costumes.

"You two girls will look so cute," she said. "Are you going to ride sidesaddle?"

"No," Holly replied. "We're going to drive in the carriage."

"With Pat and Mike pulling us," Sue added.

"What a pretty picture that will be!" Melinda said, holding a needle up to the light to thread it. "Matched ponies and matched costumes for you two girls." Then she leaned close to them and whispered, "And I bet you'll win a prize."

While she and their mother continued sewing on the costumes, the sisters busied themselves playing with scraps of material. Holly made a funny little rag-doll horse. Sue tied several bows which she planned to sew on her doll's dress.

A half hour later, Ricky burst into the room. "Hi everyone!" he cried. The women and girls returned his greeting. The boy looked at Holly. "Come on outside. I want to show you something."

"Okay," said Holly, as Sue trailed after them.

"What is it?" asked Sue, wondering if another pony had wandered into the paddock.

"I want to try an experiment," said Ricky, "and I don't want the others to know. If it works, I have a terrific idea!"

"Tell us quickly!" said Holly, excited.

In reply, Ricky led them into the stable where the appaloosa pony was quartered. All was quiet there except for the occasional whinny from a horse.

"I don't know about Stardust," Ricky announced as they reached the stray pony's stall.

"Did he get hurted again?" Sue asked anxiously.

"It's not that," said Ricky. "I just want to make sure she can really talk. I never heard of any other talking horse—not even the ones who belong to cowboy movie stars."

Holly nodded. "I've been wondering about that, too. Let's ask Stardust some questions. No one's around who could answer for her."

"I'll start," Sue said eagerly, patting the spotted pony. The small girl thought a moment then said, "What is your favorite color, Stardust?"

The pony neighed, then said, "Pink, like your hair ribbon, Sue!"

The three children were amazed. "She talks! She really does talk!" cried Holly, as Sue clapped her hands joyfully.

"Where are you from?" Ricky asked the pony.

Stardust stomped on the floor, "That's a secret," she finally said in a funny voice.

The Hollisters would have asked the pony many more questions but at that moment they heard the dinner gong ring. They hastily left the stable. While walking up to the Thomases' house, they discussed the pony.

"There's no mistake about her talking," Ricky said to his sisters. Then the boy outlined a plan to the two girls.

At the dinner table Pete said, "Pam, what are you going to do on Pony Day?"

Pam giggled. "I have a surprise." She looked at her cousin Ruth and winked.

"What is it?" Pete persisted. "I saw you take Stardust out for secret practice this afternoon. What's up, Sis?"

"I'm not telling until Pony Day," Pam replied mysteriously.

Dan spoke up, "If we find Stardust's owner first, you may not have a chance to ride her in the events."

"Oh!" Pam cried. "I hope I can go through with my surprise." But she would not tell what it was.

Mrs. Hollister asked if any progress had been made in locating Stardust's owner. Chuck told her the police had not uncovered any clues.

"We're bound to find out sooner or later,"

he said. "The owner of such a fine animal will not give up the search easily."

"I still think she might have been stolen by the men in that speeding horse van," Pete remarked, and the others agreed.

Ricky and Holly had been strangely quiet during all this discussion, and once Holly glanced at her brother and began to giggle.

"What's the big joke?" Pete asked his sister.

Her face became very red, and she answered, "You'll find out."

Then she and Ricky began to giggle so hard that their mother reminded them that it was not polite to do this at the table.

"Everybody seems to have a secret," Mr. Hollister said chuckling, "I guess I'll go get one."

Holly was afraid she had hurt him and quickly said, "You'll find out, too, Daddy!"

The children were tired from all their strenuous exercise and went to bed early. Zip, weary too from chasing small animals in the fields and woods, lay on the floor at the foot of Pete's bed. Every once in a while he would lift his head and cock his ear as if he heard some disturbing sound.

"What's the trouble, old fellow?" Pete asked him. But finally the dog settled down and Pete went to sleep. Sometime later Zip suddenly began to bark excitedly. Pete awoke at once. Between barks he could hear a noise in the stable.

"Go get him, Zip!"

In a moment the commotion outside aroused the entire Hollister family except Sue. Putting slippers and robes on they hurried out of the guesthouse to see what the trouble was.

The noise had apparently roused their cousins too. A big lamp over the main door was snapped on, flooding the place with light. At the same instant, someone dashed out of a rear door of the stable and fled among the shadows behind the building.

"Go get him, Zip!" Pete shouted, and the dog dashed toward the intruder.

A second later, everyone heard the sound of hoofs and saw a horse and rider vault a fence behind the barn. He disappeared across the fields, outracing the faithful collie. Five minutes later Zip returned, panting.

"The very idea!" Ruth said over and over. "Someone was trying to steal our horses!"

"Maybe he was after Stardust," Pam guessed. "After all, she's a valuable pony, and word may have gotten around that we have her."

"Do you suppose Sam Dulow had anything to do with this?" Ricky asked, recalling the threat the boy had made.

"From where I saw him that rider didn't look like Sam," Carol said, perplexed.

"The police are going to know about this!" Chuck said indignantly and went into the house to telephone the state troopers.

For safety's sake, Pete and Dan urged their parents to let them sleep in the barn with Zip, in case the intruder should return.

Chuck Thomas said he doubted that the stranger would return so soon. "However, if you two would like to be guards it's all right with me. What do you think John?"

Mr. Hollister gave his consent, and the boys spread blankets on the hay in an empty stall next to Stardust's. Zip nestled down between them, but the rest of the night passed without any further alarm.

When the two families gathered at the breakfast table, there was much speculation as to who the midnight intruder might have been. Some thought he was a local person, others that he had come from some distance.

"I called troop headquarters this morning, but the police have no trace of our visitor," Chuck said.

At that moment, old Ben walked in with the mail and a copy of the Central City *Herald*, a newspaper which was delivered daily to the Thomases' mailbox along the road.

Chuck excused himself to look at his letters and to read the headlines. Glancing a few moments later at the bottom of a page, he exclaimed: "Well, I'll be a monkey's uncle! Look at this!"

"What is it?" everybody asked.

Chuck gave first Ricky, then Holly a searching

stare before turning back to the newspaper. He read the headline:

"Pony to talk on TV program."

"What!" the others exclaimed.

"That's only the beginning," said Chuck. "Listen to this: A talking appaloosa pony on the farm of Mr. and Mrs. Charles Thomas will appear on the local TV station tomorrow morning."

The grownups gasped in shocked silence.

"Oh, goodness!" Ruth said. "Who arranged that?"

"We did," Holly and Ricky said proudly.

CHAPTER 13

A TELEVISION SHOW

EVERYONE burst out laughing when they heard that Stardust was to appear on television in Central City! And she was to talk! All eyes turned on Ricky and Holly, who had signed her up for the event. "Gracious, why did you do that?" Mrs. Hollister asked, amazed.

"We want to find the pony's owner," Ricky said. "It's a good way."

"Besides, she's a talking pony," Holly added, "and other children would like to hear her, too."

"Will they bring the television cameras out to Pony Hill Farm?" her cousin Carol asked.

"No, we said we'd take Stardust to the television station," Ricky explained. "Of course, we have to ask Chuck first, because he'll have to go with us. Will you, Chuck?"

Chuck grinned. "Sure. I suppose you'd call this Hollister horseplay," he said.

"And Thomas tomfoolery," Ruth added, smiling.

Holly and Ricky told how they had telephoned the television station, explaining the entire story about the stray appaloosa pony. The man was very interested and said to bring her in. If she was good he would put her on the air.

"And we're going to be broadcast over a network, too," Ricky said proudly, "on the 'Be Kind to Animals' program."

"Well," Ruth put in, "I think Chuck had better stay with you every minute on the program." She looked worried.

"Yes," said Dan. "And you'd better start very early for Central City. It's about twenty miles from here."

"May Carol and I go?" Pam asked.

"Sure," said Ricky, and Chuck nodded.

To make everyone feel better, he said he had talked to the program manager himself and assured him the talking pony was not a fake.

Chuck and the children went to the stable to prepare Stardust for the big event. Chuck told the pony what was about to happen and these words came back:

"That's fine. Thank you, Ricky and Holly, I'll do my best on television."

"See! She's happy to be a star performer," Ricky said proudly.

What combing and brushing went on for the rest of the day! Pam exercised the appaloosa later in the afternoon and rode her to a spot where no one could see what they were practicing.

Very early the next morning the pony was combed and brushed again. Chuck attached a

129

one-horse trailer to his car and backed it up to the front door of the stable.

Stardust was led from her stall by Pam and up a wooden ramp into the van. At first the appaloosa whinnied and tried to back out.

But Pam spoke to her soothingly. "Don't worry. You're about to make a lot of children happy."

Reassured by the kind girl, the pony stood quiet in the trailer. The van's door was made secure.

"Come on," Chuck said. "Jump into the car. We're off!"

Pete and Dan winked at Chuck as he pulled away. "We'll all be glued to the television set, Dad," Dan said with a grin. "I hope Stardust doesn't forget how to talk when the cameras are on her."

"I'm sure she won't," his father laughed.

The horse breeder waved and drove off. As he and the children rode along, Carol explained to the Hollisters that in order to reach the highway leading to Central City they must travel a narrow road across Great Swamp.

"It's kind of spooky along there," Carol said.

"That's only because of the stories she has heard," her father told the Hollisters. "During the Civil War some enemy soldiers hid in the swamp for a long time before they were discovered."

"Great Swamp is where Mr. Jessup saw the horse van!" Ricky exclaimed, and said maybe

130

the two bad men they were looking for were hiding somewhere in the swamp.

"Oh!" cried Pam and Carol together. Chuck told them not to worry. "The swamp hasn't been used as a hide-out for years," he said.

The children kept glancing back at Stardust to be sure she was all right. Presently they went down a long hill and onto the swamp road. On both sides were tall cattails and marshy ground. The sounds of bullfrogs, cawing crows, and wild ducks could be heard.

"It would be hard for two cars to pass here, wouldn't it, Chuck?" Ricky asked.

"Yes, but there are several turnouts made for that purpose. There's one ahead in a bend of the road."

Driving slowly around the bend, Chuck and the others suddenly gasped at what they saw before them. A *wooden barricade was stretched across the road!*

As the car approached it, two men, with handkerchiefs over their faces, leaped out and waved for Chuck to stop. Holly and Carol screamed with fright.

"Oh dear, what will we do?" Pam cried.

"Let's r-run right through the barricade, Chuck!" Ricky advised, his teeth chattering.

"I don't think I have to," Chuck replied. "I'll show these fellows a thing or two!"

The barricade was located at the turnout, and

Two men waved for Chuck to stop.

as Chuck approached it he swung sharply to the right.

"Oh, look out! We'll go into the swamp!" Carol cried.

But her father drove so skillfully that the wheels on the right remained on the road. The car, along with the van, swung neatly around the barricade. Seeing this, the two men cried out for Chuck to stop, and one of them grabbed at the tail gate of the van.

"Step on it, Chuck!" Ricky shouted excitedly, seeing what was happening.

His cousin gave the car a burst of speed, and the man tumbled off onto the road.

"We got away from them!" Pam cried out, heaving a sigh of relief.

Chuck was grim. He said nothing but paid strict attention to keeping up a fast pace until he was a good distance beyond. Then he slowed down.

"They wanted Stardust," Ricky said.

Chuck thought so too. "We're lucky," he said. "If that barricade had been anywhere else, we might have lost the pony."

The children glanced back several times, but no one was following them. Half an hour later they arrived in Central City. Chuck drove directly to the police station and reported what had happened. The captain in charge promised to send two men to the Great Swamp road immediately to look for the culprits.

Meanwhile, Pam had asked a passer-by where the television station was located, and he pointed out a tall building down the block. As the car and van pulled up in front of it a crowd of onlookers gathered.

"Is this the talking pony?" a boy asked, as the children got out of the car.

"Sure is," Ricky said.

"Then let him talk to us," the boy said.

"You go watch your television set," Stardust advised him, but would not say another word.

The watchers waited until Chuck backed Stardust out of the van. Then they scooted for their homes to be sure to watch the television program.

An attendant had come out of the front door of the building. Chuck introduced himself and the children and said, "How do we get this animal into the studio?"

"Right this way," the man replied, leading them into a side alley. "We'll take her up in the freight elevator. The studio's on the eleventh floor."

The attendant said he thought they could all get in the freight elevator, so the children followed Chuck and Stardust around to the back of the building.

Clomp, clomp, clippety, clop! The beautiful

appaloosa filly was led up a ramp and into the back door of the building. A big freight elevator, with padding around the sides, awaited them. Stardust was taken inside, followed by the children.

The elevator operator grinned and said, "I didn't think it was possible. A talking pony. Now I've seen everything."

Pam chuckled and Chuck winked at her as the elevator started up. After they had gone four floors, the light in the elevator suddenly went out and it stopped abruptly.

"Hey, what happened?" Ricky cried out.

"Everybody please be calm," the operator said. "I think we've blown a fuse."

"Let me out of here, please," Carol cried, tugging at her father's hand.

"We're between floors, I'm afraid," Chuck replied. "Now there's nothing to worry about. We'll get out of here soon."

The elevator man pounded on the door to attract attention, but there was no reply.

"We'll miss our program!" Holly wailed.

Everybody called out, but still no response.

"Great horned toads!" Chuck exclaimed. "We can't stay here all day!"

"'Course not!" said Stardust. "I need some oats!"

They all burst out laughing, and a voice from above called, "What's the matter down there?"

"We're stuck," the elevator man cried out. "Please have the superintendent locate the trouble."

A few moments later, a man called down the elevator shaft, "There's too much weight on the elevator. You blew a fuse. But we'll have it fixed in a minute."

All this while, Stardust remained calm as Pam patted her nose. "You're the most wonderful pony in the world," Holly told her.

Suddenly the light went on again, and the elevator started to rise. When it reached the eleventh floor, the operator swung open the door. Pam led the appaloosa filly out.

"Right this way. Hurry!" a man said. "It's almost time for you to go on the air."

He led the way into a studio, where white muslin carpet had been laid down. The pony walked on it over to two cameras as the director and others gathered around.

Chuck whispered something to the announcer and he nodded his head. Then he said, "This is the first pony we've ever had on television. Will you back her right over here, please?" he asked Pam.

After Stardust had been arranged exactly where the director wanted her, the cameras were aimed right at her nose.

"Now you two children stand right around here," the man said. "Our program will begin in five minutes. There's no time for rehearsal."

"Who's going to ask the pony questions?" the announcer said.

They held a quick conference and decided that Pam should be the one.

"Fine," said Chuck. "And I'd better stand alongside of you and hold Stardust so she won't move," Chuck suggested.

The Hollisters and their friends did not have long to wait. In a few minutes the announcer held up his hand. A red light blinked on.

The man looked directly into one of the cameras and said, "Today on our animal show we have an appaloosa talking pony."

Then he introduced Chuck and all the children and even told about how they had been stuck in the elevator on the way up.

The announcer turned to Pam and said, "Is Stardust ready to answer questions?"

"She is." Pam started by asking the horse her name and received a prompt reply. Then she said, "Stardust, you had an adventure on your way here today. Whom did we meet on the road?"

"Bandits!"

"What were they trying to get?"

"Me."

"Are you sure?" Pam asked. At this Stardust nodded her head vigorously, as everyone in the studio started to laugh.

"What would you like more than anything in

the world?" was Pam's next question to the pony.

"I want to go home," came the reply.

"Where do you live?" Pam asked.

"I don't remember," Stardust answered. "Will my master please come and get me?"

CHAPTER 14

THRILLS AND SPILLS

BACK AT Pony Hill Farm, Pete and Dan were sprawled on the living-room floor in front of the television set. Behind them in chairs sat Mr. and Mrs. Hollister and Ruth, laughing until their sides hurt. Sue was on her mother's lap.

"I think this is the funniest show I've ever seen!" Ruth chuckled.

As she said this, "actor" Ricky put his head close to the television camera and waved at the unseen audience. Immediately Sue slid to the floor and ran to the television screen.

"I'm going to kiss Ricky!" she cried. But by the time Sue reached the TV screen, she found herself kissing Stardust's nose instead!

Just then the beautiful pony asked if her master would come to get her. In a few moments the program ended.

An hour later the whole family assembled outside to greet the television "stars," as Mrs. Hollister called the performers. Chuck drove his car and the horse van up to the stable door and stopped. Ricky and Holly jumped out, followed by Carol and Pam.

"Oh, it was such fun!" Holly burst out. "We were nearly held up by robbers and got stuck on the elevator and everything," she continued breathlessly.

"You Hollisters certainly do bring excitement," Ruth said after hearing about their adventures. But she was alarmed at the thought of the masked men.

"Hm," said Ricky. "We got away from them easy."

After lunch Dan and Carol reminded the Hollisters that tomorrow was Pony Day. "Something exciting always happens at the events," Carol prophesied.

Just the mention of Pony Day caused the children to scramble to the stable to groom their animals. The currycombs flew. Stardust looked more beautiful than ever after Pam had rubbed her down. The Shetland ponies, Pat and Mike, were spick-and-span, as were Duke and the other horses to be shown.

After supper, Melinda came to the guesthouse, bringing the old-fashioned bonnets which Holly and Sue were to wear with their costumes.

"Oh, how quaint!" Pam said as she helped her sisters try on the complete outfits.

"Buttons, bows, and frills," Mrs. Hollister said admiringly.

"And pantaloons, too!" Pam said, as the two girls pirouetted about in their costumes.

But Sue and Holly were not the only ones planning to dress up for the Pony Day costume event. Next morning the other children went into the tack room to select their outfits.

Pam picked a white buckskin shirt and jacket with gold fringe on the sleeves and around the hem of the skirt. Ricky selected a red cowboy shirt, a green bandanna, and cowhide chaps.

"How would this white blouse look on me?" Carol said, holding it up against her shoulders.

"Wonderful!" Pam said. "And here's a green neckerchief to go with it."

Pete and Dan decided to wear broadly checkered shirts, ten-gallon hats and tight-fitting riding breeches.

"These will be best for my trick riding stunt," Dan told his cousin.

Another surprise came when the children, decked in their costumes, strode out of the stable. Their parents were waiting for them, dressed in well-tailored riding clothes.

"Oh, Mother, how lovely you look!" Pam said, running over to her parents.

"It was Ruth's idea," Mrs. Hollister said, smiling. "I understand that this is a full-dress affair."

"Mount up!" Chuck called, and everyone went for his horse.

Old Ben harnessed Pat and Mike to the carriage, and Sue and Holly climbed in. Dan was up on Duke, and Pam rode Stardust.

The riders set off for the track.

"Are you going to ride her in an event?" Pete asked his sister.

Pam smiled and replied only with, "It's a secret. You'll find out later."

Five minutes later the string of riders set off. They cut across the fields in single file, with Chuck in the lead. It was a three-mile ride to the grandstand and track where the event was held every year.

As the Thomases and their guests approached the place they met many other riders and could hear the sound of the crowd.

Then the grandstand came into view. Though it was an hour before starting time, it was nearly filled with spectators. At the center of it, and overlooking the track, riders crowded about, registering for the events.

Popcorn, ice-cream, and soda venders walked around, hawking their confections. Other men sold balloons, pinwheels, and flying birds attached to sticks. Much as the Hollister children would have liked some of these, they had no time to spare away from their animals.

When it came time for the events to begin, a tall man wearing a high hat and a long-tailed red coat walked out on the track and sounded a call on a hunting horn. This brought everyone to attention. A band began to play and everyone sang "The Star-Spangled Banner."

As the last note died away, the Pony Day

events got underway. There was a parade first for everyone, then came the trick-riding class for children of twelve or over. Dan received great applause as he somersaulted from the horse's back, ran to catch up with the animal, and leaped to its back. He won the event.

Next came the rope-twirling contest. Ricky and Carol rode side by side at a trot, spinning ropes with each hand. Another boy, who stood on his saddle twirling a rope about him and his horse, won the event. Ricky and Carol were given second prize.

As the quarter-horse race was about to start, Dan relinquished his mount to Pete. "Give him all you've got, fellow," Dan said, slapping his friend on the back.

As he did this he glanced toward the grandstand. A boy was standing there staring at them. *Sam Dulow!*

"He looks kind of lonesome," Pete said sympathetically.

"He sure does," Dan said. "I hope he gets a horse some day so he can ride in these events, too."

When Sam saw the two boys looking at him, he turned and disappeared into the crowd.

"Mount up!" Dan told Pete. "They're about to begin."

The quarter horses lined up, prancing and moving about restlessly before the starter's line.

Suddenly there came a cry, "They're off!" With a thunder of hoofbeats the horses dashed down the quarter-mile straightaway.

Pete hung on for dear life as Duke's powerful body carried him along at a terrific clip. In a few seconds the horses on either side of the boy faded behind him. Pete was in the lead!

The shouts of the onlookers rang in his ears and the wind rushed past his face. Pete flashed across the finish line to the drumbeat of Duke's flying hoofs.

"He's the fastest horse in the county!" the president of the Horse Association said as he presented Pete with a silver cup.

"I guess he is. Thank you," Pete replied. How proud he was!

Next came the costume event. What a line of young contestants formed for this one! There was an Argentine gaucho, the cowboy of South America; an Indian with war paint riding a white horse; two beautiful Welsh ponies pulling a miniature covered wagon in which sat an old-time prairie mother.

"This is a dandy show!" Pete said, sitting on his horse alongside Pam.

"Yes. And aren't Sue and Holly cute?" his sister remarked, as the girls drove along in the carriage pulled by Pat and Mike.

The little girls waved gaily as they rode past them and around the ring. As they proceeded past the grandstand, Sam Dulow suddenly jumped out from the throng and slapped Mike on the flank. Startled, the pony leaped ahead, knocking Holly off balance and making her drop the reins. Now the excited ponies dashed headlong.

"Help! Help! Get out of the way! Catch the runaways!" came shouts from the crowd as people near the track ran pell-mell out of the way of the frightened ponies.

The two girls clutched the sides of the seat as the carriage began to sway from side to side. It went part way around the track. Then, without warning, the harness broke, letting the shafts drop. The two ponies scampered off.

Holly clutched her younger sister tightly to her and closed her eyes, not knowing what would happen next. The carriage stopped abruptly near a pile of straw.

Sue and Holly were thrown into the air!

CHAPTER 15

SURPRISE VISITORS

SPECTATORS screamed and the Hollisters ran as Sue and Holly were thrown into the air. Both girls turned somersaults, but fortunately they landed right in the middle of the straw. For a moment they were lost from view, but soon their heads peeked up from the pile. In a couple of seconds they were over their fright.

"See, we're not hurted!" Sue said as her father and mother reached the sisters.

"Me neither!" Holly insisted.

As they crawled out of the straw, the two girls brushed wisps of it from their pretty costumes. Mrs. Hollister embraced them just as Ruth raced up.

"Oh, I'm so glad you weren't hurt!" their cousin said. "If you had been I'd never have forgiven myself for urging you to enter Pony Day."

Mr. Hollister and Chuck examined the broken harness. "Somebody tampered with this," Mr. Thomas said grimly, pointing out two slashes in the leather. "Could Sam have done it?"

"Maybe it was that man who was in the barn

147

the other night," said Pete, who had ridden up.

"Whoever it was deserves a good licking!" Chuck said angrily.

Dan, who had gone off after the runaway ponies, returned with Pat and Mike. By this time the little Shetlands had quieted down. Chuck meanwhile had done a temporary mending job on the broken straps. Now he harnessed the ponies to the little carriage once more.

Just then the voice of the president came over the loud speaker. "Honorable mention goes to the Hollister sisters, driving the two matched ponies."

At this the crowd cheered loudly for Holly and Sue, who came forward and made curtsies.

"And now for a surprise event," the announcer said. A hush fell over the audience as he added, "Pam Hollister and her waltzing appaloosa pony!"

How amazed her family was! So this was the secret she had been keeping! Pam rode Stardust up to the judges' stand. Then the band began to play a lovely Strauss waltz.

Guiding the pony's movements by gentle tugs on first the left rein, then the right, and a slight pressure with her knees, Pam helped Stardust perform. The beautiful filly swayed from side to side, keeping time with the music. She gracefully lifted her forefeet one at a time.

"Just like a circus horse!" Ricky cried. "How did Pam ever learn that?"

When the performance was over, the applause was tremendous. Stardust took bow after bow. The president called Pam to the reviewing stand.

"This calls for a special award," he said, handing her a trophy. It was a silver pony mounted on a metal base.

"Oh, thank you!" Pam cried. At this Stardust kneeled on her forelegs as if to thank the judge also, and again there was loud applause.

No sooner had the hand clapping died down than the voices of the onlookers rose again. Suddenly on the track appeared a girl in riding clothes standing on the backs of the Thomases' two Shetland ponies. She galloped around at a fast clip.

"For goodness sakes, it's Holly!" Mrs. Hollister exclaimed as she saw the flying pigtails.

Mr. Hollister chuckled. "That tomboy of ours is up to another one of her tricks!"

Holly had removed her old-fashioned costume, under which were her regular riding clothes. As she galloped past her family, all of them cheered and clapped.

Pam, still astride Stardust, and Pete were a little distance from the others. "We'd better help Holly get down when she finishes," said Pam, dismounting from the pony and telling her to stand quietly.

Then both children ran toward Holly, who now had slowed Pat and Mike to a trot. But she needed no assistance. Holly jumped lightly from the ponies' backs and ran toward her brother and sister, laughing.

"That was a wonderful trick," Pam praised her.

"Dan showed me how to do it," Holly replied, grinning impishly. "And Pam, who taught you to waltz with Stardust?"

"Nobody, really. One day I was humming a tune and the pony began to dance by herself, so I thought I'd try it on her back. It was easy. I guess her owner must have taught her."

Suddenly Holly gave a cry and pointed. "Look! Somebody's taking Stardust!"

"It's Sam Dulow!" yelled Pete, starting after him as Sam sprang into the pony's saddle. "Stop him!" he cried.

But it was too late. Before anyone realized what was happening, Sam had kicked the pony's sides with his heels and she had galloped off back of the grandstand.

"He's stolen Stardust!" Pam cried out.

In a few seconds Stardust and Sam were out of sight. Pete and Dan leaped into their saddles and gave chase. Chuck, who had been near by, was right after them. Two minutes later Sam disappeared into a patch of dense woods.

"We'd better not go in there," Chuck called. "It's dangerous to gallop in a forest. Our horses

"Look! Somebody's taking Stardust!"

might break a leg. Besides, Sam shouldn't run with Stardust, and if he knows we're after him he'll certainly do it."

The boys obeyed, but they felt that Sam should be caught.

"I don't think we'll have any trouble doing that," said Chuck. "Sam just let his love of horses get the better of him. We'll go to the farm where he lives and get Stardust."

When his wife heard this a few minutes later, she said, "First we'll return to Pony Hill Farm and have a late lunch. It's on our way anyhow."

"Oh, I hope Sam won't hurt Stardust," Pam worried as they rode home.

"I'm sure he won't," Ruth replied. "Even though Sam acts queer toward people, he's usually kind to horses."

When the cavalcade of riders arrived at Pony Hill Farm, they were surprised to see a strange man and a boy standing by a cart in front of the barn. As the Hollister children rode closer, they all shouted gleefully.

"Graham Stone!"

Dismounting, they dashed toward their friend, and Pete cried, "Crickets, it's good to see you!"

"We've been looking everywhere for you!" Holly told him, and Ricky asked, "How did you find us here?"

Before Graham had a chance to answer, Sue tugged his hand. "We have a s'prise for you!"

"And I have one for you, too!" the boy said. "But before I tell you, I'd like you to meet my friend Colonel Townsend."

The tall, fine-looking man with wavy gray hair and a flowing mustache shook hands with the Hollisters, who introduced the Thomases to him and Graham. The boy explained that he lived and worked on the farm of Colonel Townsend.

"Before I say anything else, though, I want to apologize for not coming to your house in Shoreham. The lawyer kept me very late and I stayed overnight with him. But I should have telephoned you."

"Did Joey Brill tell you we didn't want to see you?" Pete asked him.

Graham smiled. "Yes he did, but of course I didn't believe him."

"You weren't hiding on Blackberry Island?" Ricky put in.

"Of course not." Graham laughed. "Did Joey tell you that?"

"Yes he did," Holly answered. "And Graham, didn't you see me when you got on the train?"

"No, Holly. I heard my name called but saw nobody I knew, so I thought I was mistaken."

"We had the conductor page you at the first big city," Pam told Graham.

"I didn't go that far. I got off two stations from Shoreham to look at a horse for Colonel Townsend," the boy answered. "I'm sorry I caused you so much trouble. And now let me tell you Colonel Townsend's and my surprise."

"What is it?" Holly asked impatiently.

"Your talking appaloosa pony," Graham laughed, "belongs to Colonel Townsend!"

"What!" the children chorused.

"That's right," the man said in a pleasant southern drawl. "The filly's name is Princess. She was stolen from my farm."

Graham then told how he and the colonel had looked all over for the valuable filly but had found no trace of her until they saw the television broadcast.

"So we drove here as fast as we could," Graham said.

When he finished, the colonel smiled. "But tell me, when did Princess learn——"

At this moment, Carol, who had been twirling her lariat, tried to rope a fence post. But her hand slipped and the lasso went *whosh* right over the colonel's hat and rested on his shoulders!

Carol's face turned red with embarrassment, and she quickly apologized. Everyone else laughed, including the colonel.

"You'd be a good one to capture the horse thieves," he said, chuckling.

His question of a few minutes before went unfinished because the Hollister children were eager to tell Graham about the invention they had found inside the hobbyhorse.

"Why that's marvelous!" the boy cried after hearing the story. "By the way, I learned that my grandfather did leave everything to me, although it amounted to very little."

Colonel Townsend put an arm about Graham's shoulder and said, "That doesn't matter. Your grandfather's invention gives me an idea. But first I want to say hello to Princess."

"We don't have her!" Holly wailed, and Pam told the disturbing news of how Sam Dulow had run off with her.

"Let's go to Sam's place right away," Graham urged.

"Suppose I telephone the boy's father first," Mr. Hollister suggested.

"Good idea," Chuck agreed, and they all went into the house.

In a few minutes Mr. Hollister was talking to Mr. Dulow. "I can understand how a boy might run off with a horse as a joke," Mr. Hollister said. "And if Sam will promise not to do such a thing again, he won't be punished. We're coming over to get Princess right after lunch."

Mr. Hollister listened as Mr. Dulow replied, then frowned, saying, "He did?"

There was more conversation from the other end of the line. Then Mr. Hollister hung up.

"What's the matter, Dad?" Pam asked, when her father turned to the others. "Did Sam hurt Princess?"

Mr. Hollister shook his head. "That Dulow boy is a real problem," he said. "He brought Princess back to his father's place, packed some food into a saddlebag and then rode off again without permission."

"Where did he go?" Pete wanted to know.

"In the direction of the Great Swamp," Mr. Hollister replied.

"The Great Swamp!" Dan cried. "That's bad!"

"We'll have to go after him right away!" Chuck said grimly.

CHAPTER 16

A RISKY RIDE

"WHERE is the Great Swamp?" Graham asked after hearing that the stolen appaloosa was being ridden in that direction.

"It's about ten miles south of here," Dan volunteered.

"That's right," said Chuck. "Very few people know the trails that run through the swamp."

"I'm sure Sam Dulow does," Dan remarked.

"Yes," his father agreed.

"Dad and I know the place well," said Dan. "It's dangerous for men or horses if they get off the trails."

Chuck told of treacherous quicksands and added, "Those men who tried to stop us may be hiding in the Great Swamp. That makes it risky for Sam and Princess."

Colonel Townsend suggested that perhaps they ought to ask the police to help them with the search.

"I will if we have to," Chuck replied. "But I don't want to get Sam Dulow into any more trouble than he's now in. His parents are good, hard-working people."

The colonel nodded and added that he thought the rescue of the pony should start immediately.

"Can't we all go, Daddy?" Pam asked, tugging at her father's hand.

"Yes, let's have a real adventure!" Ricky chimed in. "I want to help find Star—— I mean Princess."

"I don't know about that," Chuck said. "If we start this late, we may be out all night."

"Hurray! A camping trip!" Dan shouted.

The grownups looked at one another. "It *would* be fun," Mrs. Hollister agreed.

"I think we could manage it," Ruth said, and the children set up a shout of joy.

"Hurry then, everyone," Chuck said. "We'll have a quick lunch, then go." To his children he added, "You know where our camping equipment is."

As the Hollister children dashed after Dan and Carol to get it, Pam said, "What'll I ride? My pony's gone."

"I'll saddle a quarter horse for you," Dan offered, "after we get the other equipment."

He led the children into the tack room. Saddlebags and sleeping sacks were hauled out of lockers by the boys while the girls gathered the cooking utensils and went to the kitchen for provisions.

In half an hour they had eaten lunch and Ben had saddled the horses and packed them. The reason for the hurried departure had been explained to him and Melinda, who would be left in charge.

Then, for the second time that day, the party of riders set off along the road.

Dan led the way, with Pete and Ricky on either side of him. Colonel Townsend and Graham, mounted on quarter horses, chatted with the Hollisters as they rode along. Chuck brought up the rear to see that no stragglers were left behind. Up and down the hills they went, stopping every once in a while to rest. Finally up ahead they saw a great, green expanse covered with some trees, high weeds and cattails.

"That's the swamp," Dan said.

His father explained that several trails crisscrossed it. "Most of the ground is low and marshy," he said, "but there's a high spot several miles from here called the Island. Dan and I went in there last year to trap muskrat."

Now the party strung itself out in single file as Dan picked his way through the tall grasses along a narrow, boggy trail. The ground would firm for a while, then slope away so that the water covered the horses' hoofs.

As they came to a muddy part of the trail, Pete pointed down and exclaimed, "Hoof marks!"

"You're right!" Dan said, "and they're fresh ones, too. I'll bet this is the way Sam came with Princess."

As word spread along the line, everyone became excited and the party pressed on faster.

"The going is easier up here a way," Dan told

the boys as they came to an overgrown road made of logs.

He explained that this old relic of a road led to the highway on the other side of the swamp. It had been built by the early settlers but was never used any more.

"It sank out of sight in several places," Dan said, "and the logs rotted."

Now, instead of riding single file, the searchers walked their horses two abreast. Suddenly Pam, who was riding behind her parents, called out, "What's that funny-looking thing in among the weeds?"

As the party stopped, Chuck came up from the rear to see what the girl was pointing at.

"Say, that looks like a—— By George, it is!" he shouted.

"What is it?" the others asked.

Chuck dismounted and pushed through the tall weeds. "It's an abandoned horse van!" he called.

The others quickly jumped down and crowded around the vehicle which Pam had discovered.

"This looks like the one which nearly sideswiped us!" Mrs. Hollister said.

"Let's look at the tail gate," Pete said excitedly. Then he added, "Crickets, it's broken."

"And there's where a splinter came off of it," Pam cried. "It must have been the very van Princess was in."

The colonel was the last one to push up alongside

"I'll bet this is the way Sam came with Princess."

the horse van. When he saw it, he gasped. "This belongs to me!" he exclaimed. "This is the van stolen from my farm when the thieves kidnapped Princess."

"Yikes!" Ricky yelled. "We're hot on the trail. Those men must be somewhere around here."

"They certainly did a neat job of hiding the evidence," Mr. Hollister remarked.

"What'll you do with the van?" Pete asked the colonel.

"Just leave it here until we return," he replied. Then he added, "That boy Sam is in real danger with the horse thieves so near."

Making their way back to the log road, everyone mounted again and continued along the trail. They had not gone far when Mrs. Hollister's horse suddenly reared up and jumped off to one side.

"What's the matter?" Chuck asked.

"A water snake just crossed in front of my horse," Mrs. Hollister shuddered.

By this time the snake had disappeared into the swamp. But as Mrs. Hollister tried to guide her mare back onto the trail, she found that the animal kept sinking into the ground. She was in a bog!

"Oh, what'll I do!" Mrs. Hollister called out.

Before the men had a chance to dismount, Ricky, Pete and Graham were at her side. Graham calmed the frightened horse while Pete and Ricky helped their mother step off onto the dry ground.

By this time Chuck had come up with a lariat.

He neatly looped it around the horse's body. Then he and Dan pulled the mired animal back onto the trail.

"It's lucky the horse didn't throw you," Ruth said as Mrs. Hollister mounted again.

"Boy, this is some adventure," Ricky cried.

"I do hope we find Sam and Princess," Pam worried as they advanced toward the center of the swamp.

"If they're in here, we'll find them," Chuck reassured her.

But the missing pony and her rider were nowhere to be seen. Meanwhile, the sun sank lower. Finally Mr. Hollister said, "Chuck, don't you think we'd better make camp soon?"

"Yes, I do."

"There's some high ground up ahead," Dan told them. "We're not far from the Island."

The horses were halted for a moment while plans were discussed. It was agreed that they could not reach the Island before dark, so they would make camp on a high spot near it.

"We'd better not build a fire," Ruth warned. "It might tip off our location to those unfriendly men."

"Then how are we going to cook anything?" Sue asked anxiously. "I want hot cocoa."

"You're right about the fire, Ruth, but I figured that problem out beforehand," Chuck smiled. "Sue, I brought a very small camping stove that doesn't give off enough light to be noticed."

"Great!" Mr. Hollister exclaimed. "I'll have to buy some of them to sell at the *Trading Post*."

Dan led the party to a rise of ground. By standing on tiptoe they could dimly see the Island, about half a mile ahead of them.

When all the camping equipment had been unstrapped from the horses and they had been unsaddled, Mrs. Hollister, Ruth and the girls started to prepare supper. The portable stove was set up, and soon the aroma of hot cocoa drifted toward the children.

"Yummie, I'm hungry!" Holly exclaimed. And the others said they were, too.

As hamburgers sizzled in a skillet, Pete began to survey the spot they had chosen.

"If you want to get a good view of the Island," Dan suggested, "stand up on your horse and look over there."

Pete flung himself on the animal and stood up, glancing in the direction Dan had pointed out. Suddenly he gave a low whistle.

"Dan!" he said hoarsely. "There's a light flickering on the Island."

"Creepers!" Dan exclaimed, and raced to his saddlebag, returning a moment later with field glasses. Handing them to Pete, he said, "Take a look with these and see if you can make out anything else."

Putting the glasses to his eyes, Pete got a very clear view of the Island in the waning light.

"It's a fire all right," he said. "I can see the smoke rising from it."

By this time, the others had gathered around the boy. Pete said he thought he could see a person among some bushes on the Island.

"It must be Sam!" Dan cried out.

"I hope so!" said Graham, looking anxiously at the colonel.

Ricky began to jump around excitedly. "Now is our chance to capture him!" he shouted.

CHAPTER 17

THE RUNAWAY

"Good!" Holly said excitedly. "We'll capture Sam and get Princess back!"

"Let's creep up on him," Pete suggested. "He's probably cooking his supper over a campfire."

Everybody discussed plans for taking Sam Dulow by surprise. Finally it was decided that the girls and their mothers would stay and guard the camp and the horses. The men and boys would proceed on foot to the Island.

"Yikes!" Ricky exclaimed, impatient to be off. "Let's go!"

Tomboy Holly did not like to be left behind and said so. But she ceased her objections when Mrs. Hollister promised a story hour before bedtime.

After good-bys had been said and the women had warned the men and boys to be careful, the searchers started off. The swamp was quiet except for the croak of bullfrogs and the occasional flutter of red-winged blackbirds disturbed in their nests. Soon it became dark.

Pete and Dan had brought flashlights, but they

did not turn them on for fear of being seen. Enough light was being shed by the moon, bright in the mackerel sky.

Squish! Squish! The trekkers' boots made sucking noises as the men and boys tramped through the soggy ground. Now Chuck was in the lead, with his son directly behind him. They crossed a very soggy spot, wading in water up to their knees.

"Ugh!" Ricky said quietly. "This is getting spookier than ever."

Reaching the other side of the watery area, Pete parted the tall cattails ahead and could see that the island campfire now appeared much closer.

Advancing further, Chuck turned around and said, "Everybody hold hands for the next few hundred feet. There are many holes in the swamp here and I don't want anyone to fall in."

The group formed a human chain and walked slowly behind Chuck.

"This is the most dangerous part of the swamp," Dan said, "but I think we'll get through it safely."

He had hardly finished saying this when Ricky walked too far to the right. With a sudden gasp he lost his grip on Pete and Dan and slipped into a water hole!

For a moment Ricky went completely out of sight. Then his head came to the surface of the water. Spluttering, he reached up with one hand. Pete and Dan grabbed it.

"One, two, three, pull!" Pete said, and in a

moment his brother was standing once more on solid ground.

When Mr. Hollister saw what had happened, he said, "I'd better take you back to camp, son. You're wet through and through and you might catch cold."

But Ricky wanted to be in on the excitement of Sam's capture. "Please, Dad, let me stay with you. I want to help rescue Princess." As Mr. Hollister considered the plea, Ricky added, "I'm only wet on the outside, Dad. That won't hurt me."

The others chuckled at this, and Mr. Hollister asked how much farther they had to go.

"Less than a quarter of a mile," Dan replied.

"Okay then," Mr. Hollister conceded. "No sense in turning back now." He took off his sweater. "Here, Ricky, put this around you."

Before they started off, Chuck warned them that from now on they must speak in whispers.

"We will," Pete promised.

They pressed on and in a few minutes came to a slight rise in the ground. It afforded a better view of the campfire. Dan, who had the field glasses slung around his neck, peered through them.

"What do you see?" Colonel Townsend whispered.

"Somebody's bending over the fire," Dan replied. "I can't see his face but he's Sam's size and build."

"Do you see Princess?" the southerner asked.

"No, sir."

Everybody took a turn looking through the binoculars at the campfire but could not spot the pony. And the person Dan had seen had moved out of sight.

"If that's Sam Dulow," said Chuck, "I'm going to talk some sense into him!"

"I guess he's alone, so we shouldn't have any trouble capturing him," Pete whispered.

Mr. Hollister thought that it would be best, nevertheless, if they crept toward the camp site quietly so as not to warn the boy of their approach.

"That's a good idea," Chuck agreed. "It's all uphill now, and the ground is dry."

Graham was the first one to drop on all fours. He led the others forward like soldiers on a patrol. Trees and bushes afforded them plenty of cover.

Soon the group was close enough to hear the wood crackling on the fire. Chuck warned everyone not to look up, as the light from the fire might reflect in their faces and give Sam a warning.

"I'll take the first peek," he said, "and tell you what I see."

Raising his head slowly like a prowling Indian, Chuck peered through the tall weeds. What he saw made him gasp and he dropped down quickly.

"Two men are sitting by that campfire!" he said excitedly.

"Where's Sam?" Pete asked.

"Tied to a tree," Chuck whispered.

"Yikes!" Ricky said unbelievingly.

They crept closer to hear what the men said.

"How about Princess?" Colonel Townsend questioned.

"She's tied to another tree near Sam," Chuck reported. "Come on! We'll creep closer to hear what the men are saying."

They pulled themselves noiselessly through the grass until they could hear the voices of the two men.

"We fooled that dumb kid good!" one of them said.

"We sure did," came the reply. "He was stupid to believe we'd buy him a horse of his own if he got Princess for us!"

Instantly, Pete realized what must have happened. These two men were the horse thieves. Princess had broken out of the van and had come to Pony Hill Farm. Then the crooks had used Sam in an effort to get the appaloosa back.

Pete crept close to his father and whispered in his ear. "Let's grab these fellows, Dad! They're the real thieves."

Just then Ricky, chilled by his ducking in the water hole, sneezed. In the stillness, the noise sounded like a cannon going off.

Instantly the two men sprang to their feet. "Someone's around. We'd better get out of here!" the taller one warned and made a dash for Princess.

"Wait for me!" the other cried, racing along behind him.

The group from Pony Hill Farm jumped from

their hiding places and dashed after the men. But by now the two thieves had reached Princess. Quickly untying her, they flung themselves on her back and galloped off down the slope. Pete and Dan were almost close enough to grab her tail, but the riders slapped her hard and she bolted off.

Colonel Townsend yelled, "Princess, come back! Whoa! Whoa! Princess, I've come to take you home!"

Hearing her owner's voice, the appaloosa stopped suddenly, and the men nearly flew off. But they kicked her sides hard, and she galloped on again.

"It's no use," said Colonel Townsend. "We'll never catch them."

Graham set his jaw firmly. "But we'll never give up until we get Princess back," he declared.

In complete disgust, the chasers halted and returned to Sam. The boys untied him from the tree. Besides being trussed up, the captive had been gagged.

When he was free of the ropes and handkerchief, Sam rubbed his wrists and ankles but would not look at his rescuers.

"Speak up!" Mr. Hollister said. "We didn't come here to punish you, Sam, just to get Princess. Tell us what happened."

Sam Dulow said he was sorry he had taken the pony. "This is how it was. I met the two men while I was tramping through the swamp yesterday looking for frogs. They said they owned the appaloosa at Pony Hill Farm and wanted her back."

"Why didn't they come for her themselves?" Chuck asked.

"They said you wouldn't believe 'em," Sam explained. "They promised me a horse of my own if I'd get Princess. That's all."

"But they don't own her," Graham said.

"Honest?" Sam asked fearfully.

"No," the colonel replied. "Who are these men? Did they give their names?"

Sam said he knew them only as Monk and Lennox.

"I thought so!" the colonel exclaimed. "The police in my part of the country have been after those two for stealing horses. They're clever. I doubt that we'll lay our hands on them in a hurry."

Sam offered to try, but Chuck said he had better come with them to their camp site.

"And anyway, we should get back to the girls."

Using their flashlights, the party made much better time returning to their camp site than they had on their way to the Island.

As they walked along, Pete asked Sam if he had cut the harness on the Shetland ponies when they were drawing the little carriage.

"No, I didn't. But I saw a mean boy from town fooling around with a penknife. I guess he did it."

There was no more conversation until they

approached the place where the girls and their mothers were waiting.

Suddenly the returning group heard cries and shouting.

"Something's happened," Mr. Hollister exclaimed, alarmed. "Hurry! There must be trouble!"

CHAPTER 18

A STRANGE CAPTURE

HEARING the cries of the campers, the men and boys raced toward the site. Had there been an accident?

Drawing closer, they could see the flickering light of a campfire. Chuck had a new worry. "Ruth shouldn't have started a fire," he said fearfully. "It probably gave away their position and the thieves are trying to steal our horses!"

"Maybe Mother is tied up the way Sam was," Ricky said in sudden panic.

Panting from their dash through the swamp, the anxious group climbed to the high ground where they had left the others.

"Great jumpin' bullfrogs!" cried Mr. Hollister, who was in the lead.

"They aren't tied up at all!" Pete shouted.

"I'll be a talking horse!" Chuck said. "Look! There's Princess!"

In the glow of the campfire stood the beautiful pony. Pam and Holly were stroking her fondly.

"Hi there!" Ruth called out as she saw the returning group.

Chuck was dumfounded. "How did you get Princess?" he cried, running up and embracing his wife. "When we heard all the noise we thought you had had an accident."

Suddenly Colonel Townsend gave a startled cry. Near him on the ground, and half hidden in the shadows, lay the two horse thieves, tied up with lariats.

"You women caught them!" cried Graham unbelievingly, and the other boys and the men stared in astonishment.

"They're the thieves all right!" Sam Dulow shouted. "The ones who got me to steal Princess!"

As everybody gathered around the two prisoners, they struggled and squirmed to free themselves from their bonds. "You can't get away," Carol said, grinning gleefully. " 'Cause girls learn to tie knots, too."

" 'Specially tomboys," Holly added.

"Tell us all about this," Mr. Hollister said when he had recovered from his surprise. "These two fellows got away from us."

"And we captured them. That's all, Dad," Pam answered as if this were an everyday occurrence.

"Who wants to tell the story?" Ruth asked gaily.

"I will," Pam offered.

As the men and boys listened openmouthed, she told how the girls and their mothers had heard the shouting on the Island when the thieves had escaped with Princess.

"You can't get away!" cried Carol.

"We didn't know what it was all about," Pam said, "but just to make sure, we hid on either side of the trail, in case anybody should come this way. Holly and Carol still had their ropes so they took them along."

"Yikes, a real Indian ambush!" Ricky exclaimed admiringly. "Then what happened?"

Pam related that when they heard the muffled sound of hoofbeats, they figured someone must be riding Princess.

"We thought it might be you boys," Mrs. Hollister put in.

"But when we saw it wasn't," Pam went on, "the girls threw their ropes."

"You certainly hit the target!" Colonel Townsend said with a chuckle.

"Oh yes," Pam replied. "Holly and Carol put the lassos right over the men's heads. Mother and Ruth helped and we dragged them off Princess."

"I don't see how you ever kept them from getting away," Graham said in wonder.

"They tried to," Pam answered, "but while Mother and Ruth held them down, we tied their ankles."

"And their hands, too," Sue yawned.

"But it wasn't easy," Carol said. Then she burst out laughing. "Mother told them if they tried to get loose, she would use a skillet on them, so they didn't move."

The colonel congratulated the captors, saying

that they had accomplished what the police of several states had been unable to do.

"And now I have some questions for you rascals," Colonel Townsend said to Monk and Lennox as he and Mr. Hollister propped the men up into sitting positions. "Why did you steal Princess from my farm?"

At first the men did not want to talk. But finally they confessed to stealing several horses in the state where the colonel had his farm. A certain circus owner, who had heard that Princess, the famous appaloosa, did a waltzing act, had tried to buy her from Colonel Townsend. When the horseman would not sell the pony, the man had engaged the two thieves to steal her.

But in driving through the countryside near Pony Hill Farm, Lennox had gone around a curve too fast. Princess had been thrown against the tailpiece and had fallen out of the van. Free, she had dashed away into the woods.

"And finally made herself at home on Pony Hill Farm," Chuck said.

Monk told them he had tried hard to get Princess back and had even prowled around the stable one night in an effort to steal her again.

"Some big collie dog chased me off," he grumbled.

"That was Zip!" Ricky burst out. "Good old Zip!"

Lennox finished the story. He had overheard plans for taking the pony to the television show and set up the road block.

"When everything failed, we got Sam Dulow to run off with the appaloosa. You know the rest."

Chuck turned to the others. "We'll go now and take these fellows to the police. We won't have to stay here overnight after all."

"Oh please!" Holly begged.

Her mother promised that they would make an overnight camping trip soon, but right now they must turn the thieves over to the authorities.

"I forgot to tell you something," Colonel Townsend said as he and Mr. Hollister laid the two men across the back of Duke, who would carry them to the nearest state-trooper station. "There's a big reward for the capture of these scoundrels."

When the camping equipment had been collected and strapped onto the animals' backs, Pam mounted Princess and Dan took the horse she had been riding. Sam climbed on with Ricky. An hour later they reached a farmhouse where a trooper lived and told their story. He took charge of the prisoners.

Then the Thomases and their guests left for Pony Hill Farm. They dropped Sam off on the way, and a little later tumbled sleepily into bed.

Ruth had insisted that Colonel Townsend and Graham remain.

The next day was one of celebration at Pony Hill Farm. Now that the horse thieves had been captured, Mr. Hollister had time to explain to Graham and Colonel Townsend the details of the hobbyhorse patents.

"Say, I know a man who could use an invention like that," the colonel said with enthusiasm. "Tell you what, Graham. I'm sure this man would buy it for ten thousand dollars. Then you can go to college and on to a veterinary school as you have always wanted to."

"That's wonderful. Thanks!" Graham said. "After I'm a vet I'll return to your farm and take care of the horses."

"Oh please come to Pony Hill Farm," Carol begged, and Graham smiled.

"And now about the reward for the capture of those villains," the colonel said. "I think you Hollister and Thomas children deserve it."

"I know what we could do with it," Pam spoke up. "Buy a horse for Sam Dulow."

"That is a grand thought," Ruth said. "I think Sam is really a good boy, and I'm sure having a horse of his own would strengthen his character."

When it was agreed that the reward money should go to purchasing a horse for Sam, Chuck telephoned the boy's house and asked him to come right over. Mr. Dulow, driving an old jalopy, arrived a while later with his son.

"If you're going to ask me to punish Sam, I believe he deserves it," Mr. Dulow said sadly.

"We're not going to punish him at all," Ruth told him. "In fact, we're going to get a horse for him."

When Sam heard about the kindness, tears came to his eyes and he quickly turned his head away so the others would not see him. But when he regained his composure, Sam thanked all of them for being so good to him.

"I'll never forget you Happy Hollisters," he said as he and his father got ready to leave.

"If you want to, you can earn the feed for your new horse by working part time for me," Chuck offered.

"I'll do it. Thank you," said Sam and, for the first time, the Thomases saw him smile.

That evening Ruth and Mrs. Hollister prepared a big outdoor picnic in honor of Colonel Townsend and Graham, who planned to leave the next morning. As big pieces of apple pie were being served at the end of the meal, the southern horseman said, "You children should have some reward for finding Princess and treating her so well. I have two handsome saddles which I will send to Dan and Carol." Then he added, "Do you Hollister children have horses, too?"

"No, but we have a burro named Domingo," Holly spoke up.

"Good!" the colonel said. "I have a beautiful donkey saddle which I bought in Mexico. It's yours."

"I know the one you mean," Graham put in with enthusiasm. "It's ornamented with imitation jewels."

"Oh, thank you, thank you!" the Hollister children chorused.

"Well, I'm glad we cleared up the mystery of the appaloosa pony before we concluded our visit here," said Mr. Hollister. "We too must leave tomorrow."

"But there's one mystery still left unsolved," the colonel said. "Who taught Princess to talk?"

"That's right," Graham spoke up. "She never did that on our farm."

Chuck looked up roguishly and rolled his eyes. "I'll have to admit to you young Hollisters," he said, "that I am a ventriloquist."

"So!" Holly said, her hands on her hips. "Then there wasn't any person at our dining-room window back in Shoreham. It was you who said we'd have fun if we came to Pony Hill Farm."

Chuck nodded.

"And you were hidden in the stable when Holly and Sue and I talked with Princess and we thought no one was around?" Ricky asked.

Chuck laughed. "Yes, and it was a good thing I was. Otherwise you wouldn't have arranged the show on TV and we might never have found the pony's owner."

Pete and Pam confessed that they had caught on to the joke early but did not want to spoil it for the others.

"Chuck," said Ricky, "will you teach me how to be a ventriloquist, so we can have a talking donkey?"

"Sure!" Chuck answered. "But that will take a while, so you'll all have to come back to Pony Hill Farm and visit us again. How about it?"

"We'll come," the children promised.

Then Sue giggled and said, "I didn't know we'd find such a 'citing mystery when we bought the hobbyhorse with the measles."